ANNE

GETTING AWAY WITH MURDER?

ANNE Morice, *née* Felicity Shaw, was born in Kent in 1916.

Her mother Muriel Rose was the natural daughter of Rebecca Gould and Charles Morice. Muriel Rose married a Kentish doctor, and they had a daughter, Elizabeth. Muriel Rose's three later daughters—Angela, Felicity and Yvonne—were fathered by playwright Frederick Lonsdale.

Felicity's older sister Angela became an actress, married actor and theatrical agent Robin Fox, and produced England's Fox acting dynasty, including her sons Edward and James and grandchildren Laurence, Jack, Emilia and Freddie.

Felicity went to work in the office of the GPO Film Unit. There Felicity met and married documentarian Alexander Shaw. They had three children and lived in various countries.

Felicity wrote two well-received novels in the 1950's, but did not publish again until successfully launching her Tessa Crichton mystery series in 1970, buying a house in Hambleden, near Henley-on-Thames, on the proceeds. Her last novel was published a year after her death at the age of seventy-three on May 18th, 1989.

BY ANNE MORICE
and available from Dean Street Press

ANNE MORICE

GETTING AWAY WITH MURDER?

With an introduction and afterword by
Curtis Evans

DEAN STREET PRESS

Published by Dean Street Press 2021

Copyright © 1984 Anne Morice

Introduction & Afterword © 2021 Curtis Evans

All Rights Reserved

First published in 1984 by Macmillan

Cover by DSP

ISBN 978 1 914150 27 2

www.deanstreetpress.co.uk

INTRODUCTION

BY 1970 the Golden Age of detective fiction, which had dawned in splendor a half-century earlier in 1920, seemingly had sunk into shadow like the sun at eventide. There were still a few old bodies from those early, glittering days who practiced the fine art of finely clued murder, to be sure, but in most cases the hands of those murderously talented individuals were growing increasingly infirm. Queen of Crime Agatha Christie, now eighty years old, retained her bestselling status around the world, but surely no one could have deluded herself into thinking that the novel *Passenger to Frankfurt*, the author's 1970 "Christie for Christmas" (which publishers for want of a better word dubbed "an Extravaganza") was prime Christie—or, indeed, anything remotely close to it. Similarly, two other old crime masters, Americans John Dickson Carr and Ellery Queen (comparative striplings in their sixties), both published detective novels that year, but both books were notably weak efforts on their parts. Agatha Christie's American counterpart in terms of work productivity and worldwide sales, Erle Stanley Gardner, creator of Perry Mason, published nothing at all that year, having passed away in March at the age of eighty. Admittedly such old-timers as Rex Stout, Ngaio Marsh, Michael Innes and Gladys Mitchell were still playing the game with some of their old élan, but in truth their glory days had fallen behind them as well. Others, like Margery Allingham and John Street, had died within the last few years or, like Anthony Gilbert, Nicholas Blake, Leo Bruce and Christopher Bush, soon would expire or become debilitated. Decidedly in 1970—a year which saw the trials of the Manson family and the Chicago Seven, assorted bombings, kidnappings and plane hijackings by such terroristic entities as the Weathermen, the Red Army, the PLO and the FLQ, the American invasion of Cambodia and the Kent State shootings and the drug overdose deaths of Jimi Hendrix and Janis Joplin—leisure readers now more than ever stood in need of the intelligent escapism which classic crime fiction provided. Yet the old order in crime fiction, like that in world politics and society, seemed irrevocably to be washing away in a bloody tide of violent anarchy and all round uncouthness.

Or was it? Old values have a way of persisting. Even as the generation which produced the glorious detective fiction of the Golden Age finally began exiting the crime scene, a new generation of younger puzzle adepts had arisen, not to take the esteemed places of their elders, but to contribute their own worthy efforts to the rarefied field of fair play murder. Among these writers were P.D. James, Ruth Rendell, Emma Lathen, Patricia Moyes, H.R.F. Keating, Catherine Aird, Joyce Porter, Margaret Yorke, Elizabeth Lemarchand, Reginald Hill, Peter Lovesey and the author whom you are perusing now, Anne Morice (1916-1989). Morice, who like Yorke, Lovesey and Hill debuted as a mystery writer in 1970, was lavishly welcomed by critics in the United Kingdom (she was not published in the United States until 1974) upon the publication of her first mystery, *Death in the Grand Manor*, which suggestively and anachronistically was subtitled not an "extravaganza," but a novel of detection. Fittingly the book was lauded by no less than seemingly permanently retired Golden Age stalwarts Edmund Crispin and Francis Iles (aka Anthony Berkeley Cox). Crispin deemed Morice's debut puzzler "a charming whodunit . . . full of unforced buoyance" and prescribed it as a "remedy for existentialist gloom," while Iles, who would pass away at the age of seventy-seven less than six months after penning his review, found the novel a "most attractive lightweight," adding enthusiastically: "[E]ntertainingly written, it provides a modern version of the classical type of detective story. I was much taken with the cheerful young narrator ... and I think most readers will feel the same way. Warmly recommended." Similarly, Maurice Richardson, who, although not a crime writer, had reviewed crime fiction for decades at the *London Observer*, lavished praise upon Morice's maiden mystery: "Entrancingly fresh and lively whodunit.... Excellent dialogue.... Much superior to the average effort to lighten the detective story."

With such a critical sendoff, it is no surprise that Anne Morice's crime fiction took flight on the wings of its bracing mirth. Over the next two decades twenty-five Anne Morice mysteries were published (the last of them posthumously), at the rate of one or two year. Twenty-three of these concerned the investigations of Tessa Crichton, a charming young actress who always manages to cross paths with murder, while two, written at the end of her career, detail cases of Detective Superintendent "Tubby" Wiseman. In 1976 Morice along with Margaret Yorke was chosen to become a member of Britain's prestigious Detection Club, preceding Ruth Rendell by a year, while in the 1980s her books were included in Bantam's superlative paperback "Murder Most British" series, which included luminaries from both present and past like Rendell, Yorke, Margery Allingham, Patricia Wentworth, Christianna Brand, Elizabeth Ferrars, Catherine Aird, Margaret Erskine, Marian Babson, Dorothy Simpson, June Thomson and last, but most certainly not least, the Queen of Crime herself, Agatha Christie. In 1974, when Morice's fifth Tessa Crichton detective novel, *Death of a Dutiful Daughter*, was picked up in the United States, the author's work again was received with acclaim, with reviewers emphasizing the author's cozy traditionalism (though the term "cozy" had not then come into common use in reference to traditional English and

American mysteries). In his notice of Morice's *Death of a Wedding Guest* (1976), "Newgate Callendar" (aka classical music critic Harold C. Schoenberg), Seventies crime fiction reviewer for the *New York Times Book Review*, observed that "Morice is a traditionalist, and she has no surprises [in terms of subject matter] in her latest book. What she does have, as always, is a bright and amusing style . . . [and] a general air of sophisticated writing." Perhaps a couple of reviews from Middle America—where intense Anglophilia, the dogmatic pronouncements of Raymond Chandler and Edmund Wilson notwithstanding, still ran rampant among mystery readers—best indicate the cozy criminal appeal of Anne Morice:

> Anne Morice . . . acquired me as a fan when I read her "Death and the Dutiful Daughter." In this new novel, she did not disappoint me. The same appealing female detective, Tessa Crichton, solves the mysteries on her own, which is surprising in view of the fact that Tessa is actually not a detective, but a film actress. Tessa just seems to be at places where a murder occurs, and at the most unlikely places at that . . . this time at a garden fete on the estate of a millionaire tycoon. . . . The plot is well constructed; I must confess that I, like the police, had my suspect all picked out too. I was "dead" wrong (if you will excuse the expression) because my suspect was also murdered before not too many pages turned. . . . This is not a blood-curdling, chilling mystery; it is amusing and light, but Miss Morice writes in a polished and intelligent manner, providing pleasure and entertainment. (Rose Levine Isaacson, review of *Death of a Heavenly Twin*, *Jackson Mississippi Clarion-Ledger*, 18 August 1974)

I like English mysteries because the victims are always rotten people who deserve to die. Anne Morice, like Ngaio Marsh et al., writes tongue in cheek but with great care. It is always a joy to read English at its glorious best. (Sally Edwards, "Ever-So British, This Tale," review of *Killing with Kindness*, *Charlotte North Carolina Observer*, 10 April 1975)

While it is true that Anne Morice's mysteries most frequently take place at country villages and estates, surely the quintessence of modern cozy mystery settings, there is a pleasing tartness to Tessa's narration and the brittle, epigrammatic dialogue which reminds me of the Golden Age Crime Queens (particularly Ngaio Marsh) and, to part from mystery for a moment, English playwright Noel Coward. Morice's books may be cozy but they most certainly are not cloying, nor are the sentiments which the characters express invariably "traditional." The author avoids any traces of soppiness or sentimentality and has a knack for clever turns of phrase which is characteristic of the bright young things of the Twenties and Thirties, the decades of her own youth. "Sackcloth and ashes would have been overdressing for the mood I had sunk into by then," Tessa reflects at one point in the novel *Death in the Grand Manor*. Never fear, however: nothing, not even the odd murder or two, keeps Tessa down in the dumps for long; and invariably she finds herself back on the trail of murder most foul, to the consternation of her handsome, debonair husband, Inspector Robin Price of Scotland Yard (whom she meets in the first novel in the series and has married by the second), and the exasperation of her amusingly eccentric and indolent playwright cousin, Toby Crichton, both of whom feature in almost all of the Tessa Crichton novels. Murder may not lastingly mar Tessa's equanimity, but she certainly takes her detection seriously.

Three decades now having passed since Anne Morice's crime novels were in print, fans of British mystery in both its classic and cozy forms should derive much pleasure in discovering (or rediscovering) her work in these new Dean Street Press editions and thereby passing time once again in that pleasant fictional English world where death affords us not emotional disturbance and distress but enjoyable and intelligent diversion.

Curtis Evans

GETTING AWAY

AT THE end of last April Robin and I embarked on our first holiday together for four years. During that time we had spent innumerable weekends in the country and there had also been periods when one of us, with time off from work, was free to spend it at home, but, owing to our careers following such divergent paths, we had rarely managed to make such interludes coincide. Now at last it had happened. Robin had three weeks' accrued leave from Scotland Yard and the powers which control such matters had indicated that the late Spring would be a suitable time for him to take it. By some miracle, the play I had been appearing in on Shaftesbury Avenue was due to close on 24th April. It had been running for six months and the London production was to be followed by a ten week tour, starting in June. So not only was I free to accompany him to whatever destination the mood dictated, but, for once, I was not beset by the anxieties usually attendant upon such freedom.

It was not all plain sailing, however, and I daresay the prospect of having nothing to do but amuse ourselves for three whole weeks daunted us both about equally. One way out of it, which each of us made a stab at, was to transform it in some fashion into a busman's holiday, although it was not immediately clear whose bus we should be travelling on.

Robin was the first to make his bid, when we were discussing where we should go:

'How about Edinburgh,' he suggested, 'as a jumping off place?'

'Brilliant!' I agreed. 'There must be more historic buildings to jump off in Edinburgh than any other city in the kingdom. Besides, why go to a city at all, when we have one all around us? I thought the whole idea was to wallow in the peace and beauty of the countryside?'

'It just occurred to me that Edinburgh might make a good base for expeditions of that kind, if you see what I mean?'

I saw exactly what he meant. He has an old friend, an ex-tutor, who now occupies a chair of something or other at Edinburgh University, a greater talker and amateur criminologist. Robin has sometimes consulted him in the past on some finer point connected with one of his cases and I had no doubt that he was hoping for the chance to do so again. I could visualise them spending long, enthralling hours together, most likely in some granite mausoleum of a club, where women were forbidden past the portals, while I carried on with the jumping off programme on my own.

'How about Paris?' I asked, staging a counter attack. 'There's always the Eiffel Tower and we haven't been there for ages.'

'No, we haven't, although it's not so long ago that I've forgotten it's also a city.'

'Oh, I know, but being abroad makes it different somehow.'

'Though perhaps not the ideal place in which to enjoy the peace and beauty of the countryside?'

'No, but the chestnuts will be out, won't they? And besides . . .'

'What?'

'There's a new play at the Champs Elysées, which has had raves. Someone told me that Derek Marsden is angling for the rights, so you never know, do you? I wouldn't half mind taking a look.'

'No, Tessa, so far as I'm concerned that's out. You know very well that my French wouldn't be nearly up to it and I'd like to remind you that the main purpose of this holiday is the one called Getting Away From It All.'

'All meaning the theatre?'

'Among other things, yes.'

I could recognise a lost cause when I saw one and resigned myself to this particular kite being wound in. Robin reciprocated by making no further reference to places north of the border and the subject of our holiday was dropped for that evening.

It was re-opened twenty-four hours later, when he brought home the news that by a startling coincidence a barrister friend of his had been telling him over lunch about a hotel called Mattingly Grange, formerly a Georgian manor house and situated midway between Bath and Taunton. The owners were a couple named Jake and Louisa Coote, the latter being distantly related to the barrister's wife, which, according to Robin, ensured our receiving special treatment, although it was hard to see from his glowing description how it could be superior to that meted out to every other guest.

It appeared that these Cootes had spent the past two years transforming the place into a paradise of comfort and taste. It was very exclusive, with only six bedrooms, and the food and wine were of the highest standards, the service impeccable and the surrounding countryside renowned for its peace and beauty.

'They keep their own horses, too,' he added, as though expecting me to find this irresistible, which I did not. However, he was so carried away by enthusiasm for the plan that I had not the heart to throw cold water on it, reminding myself that we should be putting, at most, forty-eight hours of our holiday at risk by giving it a try.

We also agreed to enter into the right spirit by observing all the conventional rules, the first of which being the unwinding process, for which Mattingly Grange sounded a better place than most. Making heavy reference to the recommendation of his illustrious friend, but none at all to his own walk of life, Robin rang up and made firm reservations for two nights and provisional ones for a longer stay.

*

It was like looking up an unfamiliar word in the diction-
ary and, having discovered its meaning, finding it leaping out
of every book and newspaper. I had gone through life to this
point without ever consciously noticing a single reference to
Mattingly Grange and yet, during the final week before our
departure, two of the people I mentioned it to had heard of
it by reputation and a third had actually been there.

This was a retired actor named Anthony Blewiston, who
I met outside a shop in Jermyn Street, where he had been
fitting himself out with a new pair of riding boots. He had
given up the stage, the better to devote himself to galloping
around in point-to-points, in the intervals between training
horses for the forthcoming National Hunt season, in both of
which he had been conspicuously successful. This could not
be said of his brief career as an actor. He had never enjoyed
life in the theatre and had presumably been drawn to it by
the need to feed himself and three horses, while possessing
no marketable qualifications beyond good looks and the
ability to mug up half a dozen lines and deliver them with
conviction, if not a great deal of sense.

However, his career had not been brought to an end by
lack of talent and application, but by a stroke of fortune in
the most literal sense. Within the past three years he had
become a man of substance. No less than two lonely aunts,
as he explained with uncharacteristic shamefaced amuse-
ment, had died, bequeathing everything they possessed to
their favourite nephew. He had retired forthwith to live off
the income on his modest estate in Sussex.

'Yes, I know the place well,' he said, as we moved down
the road to a bar of his choosing, which in itself was a
measure of his present affluence. 'Damn nice it is, too.
You couldn't do better, Tessa.'

'Well, that's good news. What is there to do there, apart from unwinding?'

'To do?' he repeated in baffled tones. 'Why, the racing, of course. What else? Isn't that what you're going for?'

'What racing?'

'Chissingfield, my dear old imbecile. You know, National Hunt.'

'Did you say Chissingfield?'

'That's right. Meetings next Friday and Saturday. If you've unwound enough by then, I may see you there. I'll have a horse entered, providing we get a drop or two of rain in the meantime. Don't want to run him on concrete. What does that faraway look in your eyes betoken? Something wrong with the drink?'

'No, there's never anything wrong with the drinks in this place, but I thought Chissingfield was in Wiltshire?'

'Quite right, so it is, now you mention it.'

'But Mattingly Grange is in Somerset.'

'Could well be, but that doesn't stop their being ten miles apart. Look at the map some time and you'll see what I mean. Oh, hang on! I do believe I'm getting it.'

'Getting what, Anthony?'

'Chissingfield is where they had that murder a couple of years ago. Right by the race course too, to add insult to injury. Oh, blind fool that I am! I see it all clearly now.'

'See what clearly?'

'This story about getting away from it all was just put out to fool the gullible public. So far from dropping the case, as we'd been led to believe, the boys from Scotland Yard are now hot on the trail of fresh evidence. Robin has been selected, and right clever thinking in my opinion, to mingle in a nonchalant fashion with the race-going crowds, posing as a harmless unwinder, with both ears cocked to pick up the vital clue. And you, of course, will be at his side to lend colour to the image. Now, own up, Tessa! Just between friends, an't I right?'

'I honestly don't know, but, allowing for a few exaggerations here and there, I have a nasty feeling that you may be. And I should have fallen for it too, hook, line and the other thing, but for this timely encounter.'

'Well, not complaining, are you? Right up your street, I should have thought. Solving the odd murder between professional engagements used to be your forte.'

'Oh, but that was different, Anthony. That was just me, the loner, prying about and asking the sort of questions that wouldn't occur to a policeman. But, if you're right, this one will be played strictly according to the rules and, believe me, I shan't be allowed within miles of it.'

'So you couldn't stop him going, even if you wanted to?'

'And I don't want to. It'll just be interesting to see how long he thinks he can get away with it. Anyway, thanks for the drink and thanks for the tip.'

'A pleasure, my dearest. I'll do my best to provide you with further instalments of both when we meet at Chissingfield. I'll probably be there, whether my little chap is running or not.'

'Good! You'll be able to tell me how I'm doing in my role of image bolsterer.'

DAY ONE

(1)

EXCEPT for the switchboard and reception desk, the lobby might have been created by a traditional stage designer as the set for an English country drawing room. There were chintz covered armchairs, faded Persian rugs on the polished wood floors and a Chinese porcelain bowl filled with tulips on a round mahogany table between the front door and french windows to the terrace.

All this looked promising enough, but, on the debit side, some of the flowers had a shrivelled look and the room also contained a watchful, yellow-eyed alsatian dog. It was posed like a Landseer lion on a rug near the desk and it acknowledged our arrival by slowly and deliberately rising on to its four legs and then remaining rigid, except for its tail, which switched back and forth in a neurotic and menacing fashion.

Ignoring it, Robin strode to the desk, whereupon the dog, evidently deciding that there was no fun to be got out of this one and that it would do better to conserve its energies for more susceptible prey, returned to its former position and transferred the baleful look to me.

Meanwhile, the tall, fair-haired young woman behind the desk remained as she had been since we came in, which was on the telephone. She was perfectly dressed to match the surroundings in a tweed skirt, pale blue pullover and single row of pearls. She looked more like the subject of a portrait photograph on page one of *Country Life* than a hotel receptionist and, although the speaker on the other end of the line was obviously one of those who needed to have her instructions repeated back to her at least twice before being satisfied that they were understood, the effect was deflating and anti-climactic. I daresay many newly arrived hotel guests who have met with a similar welcome at the end of a long journey will sympathise with the impulse which seized us both and was communicated in sign language, to pick up our suitcases and march straight out again. I cannot speak for Robin, but, as far as I was concerned, the only thing to deter me was the certainty that any such move would cause the alsatian to leap up and sink its teeth into me before I was halfway to the door.

Fortunately, the dilemma was resolved in two separate ways. The telephone conversation came to an end, enabling the receptionist to give us her attention, while behind us the front door swung open to admit another member of the cast. She entered with a crab-like movement, using her left shoulder and hip to hold back the weight of the door, both arms being needed to support a huge carton of groceries. Defying the alsatian, now on its feet again, Robin went over and held the door wide open, then took the box out of her hands.

'Oh, thanks!' she said. 'Just shove it on the table, will you. I'm Louisa, by the way, and you must be Robin Price? I recognise you by the description. And you're Tessa, of course! No need for any description there.'

These introductions concluded, she gave the alsatian a friendly, but well-aimed swipe round the ears, which sent it loping back to its place on the rug.

She was a muscular, outdoor looking woman, aged somewhere between thirty and forty, with strong man-sized hands and coarse brown hair, short and stiff as a hearth brush and, in her different style, also dressed for the part, in breeches and boots and a dark green, grubby looking jersey. She gave the impression of having come from the tractor or stables, rather than the supermarket.

'Welcome to Mattingly Grange!' she announced. 'We hope you enjoy your stay and for Pete's sake don't forget to ask for any tiny thing you need. And this here is Verity, by the way. She's helping us out during the seasonal rush. How's everything going at your end, Verity? Have you told Robin and Tessa about their rooms?'

'No, sorry, Lou, there literally hasn't been a moment to breathe. I've had Mr God's secretary on the telephone for hours about his table for lunch. He's bringing two extra, so that makes twelve. He's sorry to land you with this at the last minute, but his daughter and a friend have turned up unexpectedly.'

'Oh, Lawks! Let's keep our fingers crossed that Jake has brought back enough lobsters. Everyone's bound to want them, if they're on the menu.'

'I'll go and warn him, shall I?'

'No, don't bother, I'll see to it in a minute. Just pass over the keys for Two and Three, will you, and I'll take the guests upstairs myself. Don't worry about signing in, Robin. Any time will do and I'm sure you must both be dying to scrub up and sort yourselves out after the journey.'

'Hey, let me take that one,' Robin said, as she plunged towards the largest suitcase. 'It's much too heavy for you.'

'You'd be surprised! Still, no objection to being treated like a fragile flower for once in my life. Up we go then!' There was no lift, but numbers Two and Three were worth the climb to the second floor. They were large, airy and beautifully proportioned, with tall windows facing south over the garden, which merged into a downward sloping meadow, where sheep were grazing. Beyond that, looking tiny and toy-like in the distance, was a cluster of farm buildings, sheltered by a long low range of moss green hills. Louisa told us that it reminded her of the view from her dear old family home, where she had been born and brought up.

They were communicating rooms, with a bathroom between them, and each contained twin beds, as well as a desk, some small tables and several armchairs.

'So you can use them as bedroom and sitting room, or two bed-sitters, whichever you prefer,' she explained, scooping up a puma-sized ginger cat from one of the beds, but apparently failing to notice a vacuum cleaner standing upright in the middle of the room. 'Well, I'll leave you to it, then. Lunch is one o'clock onwards, but no hurry. We want you to relax and enjoy yourselves. And don't forget to let us know if there's anything you need.'

'Odd, isn't it?' Robin remarked a few minutes later, having spent the interval staring out of the window. 'Almost unique, I shouldn't wonder.'

'Oh, I don't know,' I said, my own interval having been spent in transferring the vacuum cleaner to the landing and inspecting the built-in cupboards, 'a trifle slapdash and eccentric, perhaps, but I find that's often the case with animal lovers.'

'I was referring to the view, as it happens. Had you realised that what we are looking at now must be exactly the same as was seen by the people who lived here two hundred years ago?'

'No, it isn't. The farm buildings would have been quite new in those days. Some of the trees hadn't been planted and the rest would have been about half the height they are now. And had you realised, Robin, that we've only been given four coat hangers between us?'

'No, my mind was on higher things, but four is the most I'll need and I foresee no difficulty in getting another four dozen for you. I hope that carping note doesn't mean that you've made up your mind to dislike the place?'

'No, I'm keeping an open mind. On the whole, I'm in favour and I think we should take Louisa's advice and scrub up in good time for lunch.'

'She also told us there was no hurry and that we were to relax.'

'I know, but it's ten to one and I worry about Mr God. We don't want him and his eleven archangels scoffing all the lobster before we get a look in, do we?'

(2)

'I don't feel so keen to get to heaven, after all,' I remarked during lunch. 'He looks reasonably benign, and I didn't expect a flowing white beard, but spectacles, even gold rimmed ones, and that paunch are rather a let-down. I find the entourage disenchanting too.'

'His name is Denzil Godstow,' Robin said, 'as I discovered during my session in the bar, while you were putting the finishing touches to sorting yourself out.'

'Oh, I see! So that makes it all right for him to have a daughter. What else did you discover? Is he a local?'

'Not a real one. According to Kenneth, the barman, he owns a small palace about three or four miles away, but he only uses it for the racing.'

'So that disposes of another puzzle. I'd been wondering what Jock Symington was doing in celestial company.'

'Which is he?'

'The florid one, sitting next to the girl in the yellow suit, who is Miss God, if appearances don't deceive. Her name is Diana, and the blonde giggler with her back to us, who they call Stephanie, must be her friend. I've a feeling I've seen Diana somewhere before, but I can't place it.'

'But I take it you have met Jock Symington?'

'No, never, but he's a very successful trainer and he's often on television before the big race, explaining why his horse has the best chance of winning it. He's not always right, though. Did Mr God get his name for brevity's sake, or because he behaves as if he were?'

'A bit of both, I gather. He looks quite ordinary and unassuming to me, but perhaps money does the talking for him.'

'No doubt, and ruthless with it, I shouldn't wonder. Those quiet ones are often the most dangerous. Let me have rich men about me who show off and I know where I am, but I shouldn't care to get on the wrong side of this one.'

Curiously enough, a moment later someone may have managed to get an inch or two on the wrong side of him, although I do not believe it was intentional. More curious still, Robin and I were partly to blame.

I had been observing Mr God from time to time while we talked and now saw him raise his hand, not as though signalling to the waitress, but in the style of one waving to an acquaintance, to whom he was prepared to grant audience. Looking round, I saw that the chef, in full regalia, was standing in the doorway, casting an appraising eye round the room. Then, without appearing to notice the invitation from the biggest spender present, he came across to our table and introduced himself:

'Hallo! I'm Jake and I just looked in to say I'm delighted to see you both. Everything all right?'

He was a tall, thin, sad-eyed and nervous looking man, with a long nose and chin. It was impossible to tell whether the upper part of his head was in proportion to the rest because his white cap was a size too big for him and came down over his eyebrows. His manner was awkward too and, although doing his best, he gave the impression that this kind of public relations bonhomie did not come naturally to him.

To console him, and because Robin seemed to have been rendered temporarily speechless, I said effusively:

'Oh, terrific, thank you. We both adore lobster and these were really special.'

'Yes, well, get them straight off the beach, kind of thing, and bring 'em back alive, so we do know they're fresh. Glad you liked them and hope you enjoy your stay. Don't forget to let us know if there's anything you need.'

Then, with the relieved air of having done what was required, he left us to return to his own regions, without so much as a glance at the big table in the centre of the room.

I was unable to gauge Mr God's reaction to this snub, if such he considered it to be, because my full attention was now focussed on Robin. I rarely see him fazed, but it had not escaped me that he had remained completely dumb in the presence of Jake and had looked at least as relieved to see the back of him as Jake had been to present it.

'I suppose you're wishing he hadn't done that?' I suggested.

'Done what?'

'Poured incense all over us.'

'Not at all. I enjoy tripping down the red carpet on the rare occasions when it's unrolled for me.'

'Only this time I had the impression that you were hoping to pass yourself off as Mr Everyman and not be singled out for special attention?'

'Well, it was unexpected, I grant you, and I may not have responded with all the same gush and saccharine as you manage to throw around on these occasions, but that doesn't happen to be my style. I am sorry if it offends you.'

'Not in the least. I was only sounding you out.'

'What about?'

'Whether you've unwound enough to tell me why we really came here?'

'Oh, honestly, Tessa, do we have to go through all that again? I can't think why you go on about it and it's not like you to take a dislike to something for no reason. The place seems to me to offer more or less what we were looking for, but obviously there's no point in staying, if you're determined to find fault with everything. If you want to move on, why not just say so?'

'And then what?'

'We'd move on, of course.'

'Would we really?'

'Well, perhaps not today or tomorrow. It's not exactly cheap, as you know, and we've made firm reservations for two nights, so we're stuck with that. But I daresay you could put up with it for another forty-eight hours? At least, you won't starve.'

'I'll put up with it for as long as you like, Robin. I don't deny that it has a lot to recommend it, but I feel I'd enjoy it so much more if you were to tell me what's going on.'

He was able to put off replying for a minute or two, because a trolley had been wheeled up to the table, allowing him to plunge into a flurry of indecision between the chocolate pudding and strawberry flan, although it was clear to me, if not to the waitress, that he had little intention of taking either.

'No, after all, I shall follow your advice, Tessa, and restrain myself. Just coffee for two, please!'

'That was not my advice,' I reminded him while we waited for it to come. 'On the contrary, I've been urging you to let yourself go.'

'I know that, and how the hell you've managed to catch on to what's been going on in my mind is something I'll never understand. You have been referring, of course, in your oblique way, to the Chissingfield case, in which I came such an almighty cropper two years ago.'

'Going on in your mind, did you say?'

'Yes, of course. Where else?'

'Not, by any chance, an assignment, with official backing and co-operation?'

'Good God, no! And isn't that typical? By some fluke, you get hold of the glimmerings of the right idea and then your feverish and twisted imagination goes to work and transforms it into something unrecognisable. In fact, you may be interested to hear that the reason why I didn't want to discuss it was that for me, at any rate, the unwinding process seems to have taken hold somewhere between Hounslow and Maidenhead. By the time we arrived here I was ready to drop the whole silly idea of harking back to the past.'

'You honestly mean that?'

'Yes, I think I may have matured a bit during the last sixty or seventy miles. While I was standing by the window just now and looking at that view, it hit me that things had come to a pretty pass if, with all that around me, I could still allow three-quarters of my mind to dwell on unsolved crimes, long forgotten murders and all the other squalid clutter that fills my working days. I decided it wasn't fair to you and it wasn't good for me and the time had come to snap out of it.'

'And I think you were wise.'

'Good! Subject now closed.'

The coffee had arrived and while we were drinking it I said: 'The only thing that bothers me is how far you'll succeed in sticking to this sensible resolution. I have a suspicion that it takes more than a flock of sheep on a sunny morning to change one's outlook on life and send all the built-in disciplines packing.'

'This will be a new sort of discipline and I mean to have a damn good try.'

It was now beginning to sound more like a spiritual exercise than a pleasure trip and I was at a loss to understand how he expected to enjoy his holiday by turning it into a private battlefield. However, I accepted it as a passing phase in the early stages of unwinding and changed the subject:

'They're leaving now and Mr God has signed the bill without so much as a glance. How far would you say this has set him back?'

'Quite a lot, judging by the à la carte. He wasn't drinking wine himself, I noticed, but some of the others more than made up for that, notably your Mr Symington. Something between three and four hundred, I daresay.'

'Oh, my goodness!' I said, throwing a lot of horror and disgust into it, although in fact I was not displeased. It was a comfort to discover that Robin still had some way to go before he became so unlike himself as to fail to keep a critical eye on the behaviour of those around him.

(3)

Back in Numbers Two and Three, which were rapidly becoming our home and refuge, we debated for a while whether to work off the post-luncheon lethargy by going for a walk, or to surrender to it and collapse. Our physical and mental states making such decisions hard to arrive at, we agreed to toss for it. Robin flipped a coin in the air, but I cannot remember whether it came down heads or tails. I think we may both have been asleep before it fell to earth.

The next three hours provided a fine example of the snares that lie in the path of those attempting to break out of the routines which circumstances have imposed on them. Over the years, I have trained myself to drop in and out of cat naps and siestas, where and when I could. It has become second nature to me now, but things are different for Robin. He so rarely finds an opportunity to sleep in the afternoon that when he does so the alarm clock inside his head has a way of losing its bearings and concluding that it must be the middle of the night.

So, after two frustrating, wakeful hours, I decided not to waste any more of the holiday, but to set forth and explore the countryside on my own.

*

The lobby was deserted. No Verity behind the desk nor, I was thankful to see, an alsatian in front of it, so I availed myself of the opportunity to glance through the Visitors' Book.

The most recent entry was Robin's and no one else had checked in on that day, although a Mr and Mrs Fellowes had arrived on the Saturday before. I assumed them to be the elderly couple I had seen in the dining room, who had marked themselves out as residents by not waiting to be directed to their table. The entry above theirs was dated a week earlier.

This information was somewhat at odds with a remark of Louisa's, for it hardly measured up to the accepted idea of a rush period. However, I concluded that we were now in the lull before the racing weekend storm and that Verity had been recruited in advance to be groomed for stardom.

It was also a disappointment to discover that the elderly couple were only plain Mr and Mrs. In the brief intervals between listening to Robin's true, if grudging, confessions and keeping tabs on Mr God's party, I had been able to spare a modicum of attention for the Fellowes and to play the guessing game about their relationship and background. The first had presented no difficulty because people who have been married for a long time often have a way of speaking to, while not looking at, each other, which had been the first give-away. The rest was harder to establish, but on the whole I had been inclined to put him down as a retired ambassador or governor-general. Although probably in this mid-seventies, he was tall, stately and upright, with snow-white hair and noble features, all of which made it easy to picture him taking the salute in his fancy dress on state occasions. Furthermore, his complexion, in contrast to the hair, indicated long sojourns in tropical climes. The fact that his wife had pale hair and a junket-coloured complexion did nothing to interfere with this image, because that is the unfair effect which the same tropical climes often do have on women. Also, although superficially unostentatious in every way, there was poise and self assurance in her bearing and I could just imagine her putting the junior diplomats' wives in their places with the gentlest and most deadly of rebukes.

However, had my guess been right, a KBE must surely have been the least of the handles he would have acquired along the way, so, for want of better employment, I was setting myself to rearrange Mr Fellowes's career for him, as I walked, by way of the french windows, on to a brick terrace, from where the garden sloped down to meld with the meadows stretching away into the distance.

I had reached the point of re-casting my hero as an old style explorer or anthropologist, setting up camp in the African swamps, with Mrs Fellowes treating the babies for colic and converting the cannibals to vegetarianism, when the train of thought was broken by the sight of another human being striding up the lawn towards me.

This was Verity and she had the alsatian on a leash, although, as they came nearer, the impression grew that the alsatian had Verity on a leash, for he was straining forward like a dog possessed and she appeared as helpless to restrain him as if he had been a tank in top gear. Since he was obviously making for the house, I could not understand why she did not drop the lead and let him get on with it, until it struck me that he might be making for me, in which case I had cause to be grateful to her.

'Hallo, there!' she said, when she had flopped into a basket chair and recovered some of her breath having, to my relief, hooked the lead round an iron table leg, leaving the alsatian on the other end of it. 'Are you all right? Anything you need?'

'No, thanks awfully, everything's fine. I was bracing myself for a stroll round the garden.'

'Oh, good! I saw you come out and the staff have a way of evaporating during the afternoon, so I thought I'd better dash up and do my stuff.'

'How very kind of you! I'm sorry to have interrupted your walk.'

'Oh well, you see, one of my jobs is to give this brute some exercise, when I can fit it in, but of course he didn't fancy coming back when we'd hardly gone a hundred yards, so I put him on the lead and you saw what happened then? Almost went berserk. He really is retarded, that animal. Anyway, he's had his lot for today. I've done my bit.'

'I don't imagine there are many receptionists who'd consider it their job to take him for walks at all. Your union must be slipping.'

'Oh, I don't mind, when he behaves himself. It's an excuse to get out of doors and I need the exercise just as much as Fido here. You can't let a dog with his IQ go roaming off on his own, with all those fat sheep just waiting to be chased. And Louisa and Jake haven't time to do much about it. They're rushed off their feet, as it is.'

'Oh, are they?' I asked, twisting my head round to glance at the deserted rooms behind me. 'I was beginning to wonder if they'd evaporated too.'

'Oh Lord, no. Lou's taken the Land Rover into Chissing-field to pick up some compost Jake needs for the garden. They grow all their own vegetables, you know. It's one of their proud boasts.'

'Is that what he's up to now? Hoeing the lettuce bed?'

'No, actually, he's restoring the summer house to its full glory. It's down there, past the stables on the left, behind that great clump of rhododendrons. I don't think you can see it from where you're sitting, can you?' she asked, springing up and stationing herself behind my chair. 'No . . . well, that is, not if you're sitting down, I imagine.'

'I can just see a bit of roof, now that you've pointed it out,' I told her, wondering why she was making so much of it.

'If you're going for a stroll, you could do worse than make that your objective. It's really awfully charming and Jake would be glad of a chat to break the monotony. I wasn't much use in that way. I did look in for a moment, but I couldn't stop because my intuition told me that at any moment Towser would take it into his head to knock the tin of creo- sote over and start paddling his great paws in it.'

'What's his name really?'

'Lupus. Known to some as Loopy. Not that he answers to either, I might say. Well, I mustn't keep you from your walk. Your husband's evaporated too, I take it?'

'Yes, but I think he might be ready for a cup of tea by now, if you could organise it?'

'Shall be done,' she answered, stooping down to unhitch the lead. 'You may depend on me.'

'How's it going?' I asked from the doorway of the summer house, which was not so strikingly charming, after all. 'Oh, sorry! Am I blocking your light?'

'Not to worry, I've almost done now. Just got to finish undercoating this window and then I can leave it to dry out.'

I had been hoping to see what he looked like without his chefs uniform, and was disappointed to find him now wear- ing an overall over dungarees, an old felt beret stretched down over his ears and a pair of household gloves. I assumed that the purpose of all this protective clothing was to prevent him from smelling like a walking paint pot when he got to work on the fillet of beef and *sauce béarnaise*.

'Is there anything you need?' he asked.

'Only to see how you're getting on. Verity thought you might be in the mood for company.'

'Yes, I saw her out there in the garden, at one point. Out on her rounds with old Loopy, I expect.'

'That was the intention, but she'd only just started out when she saw me and came all the way back to see if there was anything I needed. I must say, you're all very attentive.'

'We aim to please,' he said, attacking a blob of paint which had landed on the window pane.

'And succeed, I imagine. Most people love to feel cosseted. I'm sure it pays off?'

'We have our ups and downs, like everyone else, I suppose.'

'Have you been in the business long?'

'Not here at Mattingly. We only bought this place two years ago, when it was falling down from neglect, and spent about six months working on it before we opened.'

'That was pretty good going, wasn't it, if it was really in such a bad state?'

'Well, luckily, the plumbing and wiring had been modernised a few years before. I imagine that's when the owners ran out of money and had to sell up. Anyway, it meant that we were able to do most of it, decorating and conversion and so on, in our spare time. Still at it, actually, as you can see.'

'Where were you before that?'

'Little pub called the Weston Arms, on the outskirts of Chissingfield. That was another run down place.'

'And did you do that up too?'

'Not on anything like the same scale. It was only a tiny place. Attractive, in its way, but they'd had a succession of rotten landlords, including a couple of alcoholics, which is an occupational hazard in our line of business. Anyway, it was losing money, so the brewery sold it off as a free house, if you know what that means, and we stepped in.'

'And transformed it into a going concern?'

'We did pretty well, yes. We turned one of the bars into a restaurant and started serving lunch and dinner to the carriage trade. The word got round and there wasn't any competition to speak of. In next to no time we were serving two sittings at dinner and packed out every night of the week.'

'Must have been hard work?'

'Yes, it was tough going, but we worked as a team and Lou took care of all the business end. That's her strong suit.'

'How long were you there?'

'Couple of years. Good years they were too, in a way. Then this place came on the market. We were about ready to spread our wings, by then, and Lou'd always had dreams of taking on something really big and making it into a four star de luxe hotel. The pub was worth three times what we'd paid for it, so it seemed the right moment to move on.'

'And it's been a huge success, I'm told.'

'Like I say, we have our ups and downs. For one thing, to run a place of this size you need staff and that brings problems we hadn't had to deal with before. The horses take a lot of looking after, too. Still, we get by and Lou takes care of all the management side, among a lot of other things.'

'And of course it must be an advantage to have stayed in a neighbourhood where you were so well known? I expect a lot of old faithfuls still rally round in your new splendour?'

'Some do, but loyalty cuts both ways, you know. This is very up-market, compared to the last place, and lots of people prefer that cosy, informal atmosphere. Suits their pockets better too, in these hard times.'

He was now engaged in the task of cleaning brushes and replacing lids on the paint tins and, realising that my time was running out, I said:

'I suppose you must have been in the thick of it when they had that murder in Chissingfield a few years ago?'

'Oh, that! The race course murder, as the popular rags used to call it. Yes, it was quite soon after we took over the pub. Bit of a bonus, really. The public bar was packed out every night with people exchanging the latest rumours. Got us off to a good start, in a way. Was your husband concerned in that one?'

'Yes, but he'd rather not think about it. One of his few failures, I'm sorry to say. As you probably remember, they never discovered who did it, although I bet a lot of people round here had their own ideas about that, didn't they?'

'Expect so. Can't remember all that much about it now. Four years is a long time. Which reminds me: you wouldn't happen to know what time it is now?'

'Twenty to six.'

'Then I'd better get moving. Thanks for dropping in. Enjoy your walk and don't forget to let us . . .'

'I won't,' I promised, before he could complete the tag line.

(4)

Robin was emerging from the shower, having drunk the tea, which Verity had brought up to him in person and, to my critical eye, appeared to be in a less aggressively relaxed mood than when I had last seen him.

'Where did you go?' he asked.

'Only to the summer house and back.'

'What's special about the summer house?'

'Nothing much, but there's a lot going on there. In fact, you'll be relieved to hear that you're no longer in immediate danger of being urged to behave as nature intended you to. You may surrender to the joys of the pastoral scene and to repairing the ravages to your soul and I shall not complain. Dismiss all thoughts of getting and concentrate on spending.'

'Thanks. What's brought this on?'

'I have stumbled on a little mystery of my own. Very prosaic, I'm afraid, but perhaps my feverish imagination will be able to twist it into something more sensational.'

'Yes, well, you must tell me about it some time, but first I want to apologise for the bad tempered things I said at lunch. I didn't mean half of them, but the fact is that when you started going on about the Chissingfield murder, I'd just had a most unpleasant shock and I wasn't sure how I was going to handle it.'

'What shocked you?'

'I'd recognised someone. And that wasn't the only thing to rock the boat either. I had begun to feel that the Furies were gathering.'

'Someone in Mr God's party?'

'As a matter of fact, it was Jake. He was one of the people I interviewed.'

'Are you sure, Robin? He didn't seem to remember you.'

'I wonder? I had the impression he was just as thrown as I was. Probably like me, better at faces than names, and I certainly haven't forgotten his. Curiously enough, it was that outsize cap which clinched it. It had the effect of emphasising the long nose and chin, which is what I remember most clearly about him.'

'It's odd,' I said, 'but I hadn't connected until now, but of course, you're right, he must have recognised you. When I was talking to him in the summer house, I mentioned the murder and he asked me if you'd had anything to do with it. But when you booked our rooms you just gave your name and no other details, so it can only have been when he saw you in the dining room that he realised who you were. And, as you say, he did give the impression of being knocked all of a heap. Although he wouldn't have any reason to feel alarmed at meeting you again, would he?'

'None whatever, as far as I know. That's mainly what fidgeted me. I saw the flash of recognition and I was waiting for him to say "Well, fancy meeting you!", or something of the kind. After all, he was only one of scores of witnesses who had to be worked through in the early stages in his case, simply by virtue of his job, which brought him into contact with so many people in and around Chissingfield. But instead of behaving naturally, he looked guilty and uncomfortable.'

'You may be making too much of it, you know. Perhaps he felt a bit of a fool trying to carry off his maitre d'hotel act with someone who'd known him as a humble publican. It's not surprising that you should have jumped to the wrong conclusion, because it's been so much on your mind just lately, but I daresay it's only a vague memory to him. It was nearly four years ago, after all.'

'No, it wasn't. Not much more than two.'

'Oh, are you sure?'

'Of course I am. It's not the kind of mistake I'd be likely to make.'

'So what do you mean to do about it?'

'Nothing whatever. There's nothing I could, or wish to do about it. I was simply offering an excuse for my bad temper. I was annoyed with him and with myself and I took it out on you.'

'Well, that's very handsome of you, Robin, but you really shouldn't blame yourself for feeling annoyed by the fact that someone from your unhappy past is now bobbing about, looking guilty and begging you to let him know if there is anything you need. It would be enough to get anyone down.'

'The trouble is, my dearest, there is something I need, only it's not in his power to provide it.'

'What's that?'

'I want him to go away and stop reminding me of events which I am trying to forget. His mere presence undermines my good intentions, or, rather, forces me to recognise what frail foundations they were built on. As soon as I saw him, my mind ceased to dwell on sheep and chocolate pudding and how it would feel to be as rich as Mr God, and slid back into its everyday groove. However, I won't be beaten. I mean to rise above it.'

'Okay, so what shall we do this evening, to send the ghosts on their way? How about driving over to Bath for dinner? There might be something on at the theatre?'

'That's not what I call beating it, that's just running away. Besides, you seem to forget that I don't know how it feels to be as rich as Mr Godstow and our terms here cover full board and lodging. Everything included except wine and spirits.'

'Oh, all right, but that doesn't mean that we have to hang around waiting for the next fully paid up meal. I know, let's go for a drive and find some picturesque pub, where we can drink our wine and spirits without wasting a penny and still be back to claim our money's worth at dinner.'

'There could be another way of tackling the problem, you know,' I remarked, as we sat facing each other across a picturesque and rickety wooden table in the garden of the Rose & Crown at Middle Hinkley, which happened, although obviously this had nothing to do with running away, to lie eight miles in the opposite direction from Chissingfield. 'What you might call the psychiatric approach.'

'Oh, you think I'm ready for the couch now, do you?'

'Why not? It has been known to work and all you have to do is spill it out in any old order and, when you've parted with the last little secret failure, you'll be a free man. It ceases to be your problem and you listen with lofty detachment while someone else explains the whys and wherefores.'

'Someone like yourself, for instance? I must tell you that it wasn't quite my understanding of how the treatment works. I thought it took months, or even years, to dig out the last buried secret. And then, after all that effort, it turns out to derive from some unhappy experience in my childhood, like being shut in the broom cupboard.'

'That's precisely what we need to find out.'

'No, we don't. I had an idyllic childhood and the only thing that bothers me now is that, somewhere, there is someone who committed a vicious and brutal murder, for which he will never be called to account and that it is partly my fault. And what on earth would be the point of dragging that up again? You must remember the case almost as well as I do?'

'No, I don't. I've had a lot of other. . . . I mean, you've been involved in a lot of other tricky cases since then and I sometimes get them mixed up. Four years, after all . . .'

'Not four years, two.'

'Oh yes, I keep forgetting. All the same, two years is a long time to remember all the details, so why not humour me and give it a try?'

'Two years ago last February,' Robin began in a parrot-like voice, 'a girl called Pauline Oakes, a hard-working, nice-looking, serious-minded young woman, who worked for a firm of estate agents, was found murdered on the heath by Chissingfield race course.'

'Who found her?'

'A woman named Eve Pollock, who had been almoner at Chissingfield General Hospital. On her retirement she had moved into a bungalow on a housing estate overlooking the race course, and she made the discovery one morning when she was exercising her dog. To be precise, it was the dog who made it. Pauline was not then visible to the human eye.'

'You mean she'd been shoved into some bushes, or something?'

'No, that isn't what I mean. She was lying on open ground, covered by a tarpaulin, where she'd been for exactly ten days.'

'But even between meetings there must be people about, the clerk of the course and groundsmen, for instance. So, if she was on open ground, why hadn't someone found her before? And, if not, how was it possible to tell how long she'd been there?'

'It was like this. Friday, the 10th of February that year was the opening day of Chissingfield's biggest National Hunt meeting of the season. It attracts people from all over the country arid weather conditions were so chancy at the time that some of them played safe and arrived the day before. So by Thursday evening the town was beginning to fill up. As it happened there was only a slight snowfall that night and when the stewards made their last inspection of the course on Friday morning, they gave the go-ahead. The first race went off according to schedule and was notable in two respects. One was that the odds-on favourite, with the champion jockey on board, was beaten by a twenty-to-one outsider.'

'It can happen.'

'In this case, there was a stewards' enquiry, complete with patrol camera and all the rest of it, as a result of which the losing jockey was hauled up and reprimanded for dropping his hands fifty yards out from the post.'

'And did the favourite and the lucky outsider come from the same stable, by any chance?'

'I always forget how knowledgeable you are about the seamy side of racing.'

'It's just that I remember something like that happening once at Lingfield. I'd backed the outsider that time, simply because it was called Gala Performance, but it was a real turn up for the book and it made a lasting impression on me. You wouldn't happen to remember your trainer's name, I suppose?'

'As though you hadn't guessed! I've told you already that I'd had a minor setback before Jake came prancing up and delivered the knock out. I'd almost got over it by then, too. Reminded myself that it was only natural that Symington should have friends and connections in this neighbourhood and that it wasn't his fault if his presence in the dining room brought back memories I'd been striving for the past two hours to bury.'

'It's a pity I told you who he was. Still, it's done now. What else happened in the first race?'

'You asked me how it was possible to establish to within hours when Pauline was killed, after such an interval?'

'Yes, I did.'

'And, if you have also been wondering why there should have been such an interval at all, the answer to all three questions is the same. It had started to snow again by the time the riders got up to the start. Twenty minutes after it was over, and while the enquiry was still going on, it was falling so thickly that visibility was down to a few yards and the meeting was abandoned. It went on snowing through-out the whole of Friday and that night a hard frost set in. This pattern was repeated without a break for over a week.'

'I begin to get the picture.'

'And what a picture it was! I daresay the people round here will be talking about it for years to come. Hundreds of sheep were lost, and just travelling from one point to another, either on foot or by car, became a major oper-ation. Every day a fresh layer of snow falling on a layer of frost before there'd been time for it to melt, to be followed by another frost as soon as it got dark.'

'And this went on for ten days?'

'Not quite. On the ninth day the wind changed and conditions began to improve. By the 20th of February the thaw had well and truly set in. The ground was still blanketed in snow, but the trees no longer looked like abandoned igloos and Miss Pollock ventured out with her dog on their favourite walk across the heath which separated her garden from the race course.'

'Although I imagine it is not her favourite walk any longer?'

'Probably not, but we had reason to be grateful to her for braving it then. Another twenty-four hours of steady thaw would have changed everything. As it was, the state of that patch of ground where Pauline was lying proved beyond doubt that she had been there since the first snowfall. Nature, if you will forgive the whimsy, having obligingly encased her in its very own deep freeze before rigor mortis set in, it was possible to establish the date, almost the hour of her death.'

'Yes, I see!'

'Unfortunately, that was the first and only break to come our way and it opened up such an enormous field for investigation as to make the task hopeless from the outset. Two or three hundred nameless, faceless potential suspects, all able to claim a valid reason for being in Chissingfield on that evening and all of whom had melted back into their unknown backgrounds ten days before anyone knew there'd been a murder. I ask you!'

'But you were able to eliminate all the local people?'

'Well, I suppose it could never be said that it wasn't one of them, but after three or four weeks of unremitting slog, following up every tiny lead that came our way, we had to give up on that one. Pauline appeared to have no enemies, no broken or unbroken love affair; no one in her circle with a history of violence and there had been no previous attacks of that nature within living memory. So it must have been an outsider and I have as much chance of finding out now who he was as I had two years ago. Which is why I had begun to realise what a fool I was to try and put the clock back, when we're supposed to be here to relax and enjoy ourselves.'

'All the same, Robin, there must be more to it than you've told me. Ten days is a hell of a time for someone to be missing, and not even presumed dead. What sort of a girl was she, this Pauline, apart from being serious-minded and hard-working?'

Robin glanced at his watch: 'Fillet of beef, did you say?'

'That's what I saw on the card when I was snooping around during your siesta.'

'Well, we don't want that to be overcooked, do we? Perhaps we'll talk again about Pauline, but for the moment I'll leave you with one fact, which will interest you. She was someone who had a phobia about horses and everything connected with them. For which, I might add, she had the best of reasons.'

(5)

I tried to get him to enlarge on this statement on the drive back, but he would not be drawn.

'No, Tessa, one session on the couch will do for today. In fact, one may be all I needed. I suppose that deep down in my sensitive soul, I'd been haunted all this time by the fear of having left undone something which ought to have been done, but your treatment has done the trick. I can see now how vain that was. Admittedly, it turned out not to be enough, we did the best we could and lack of supernatural powers is nothing to kick oneself about. So I'm grateful to you and you shall have your reward. Let's swop roles and you tell me about that other mystery you referred to before we got bogged down in mine. With any luck, it'll turn out to be a lot more amusing.'

'No, even more flat, stale and unprofitable, I'm afraid. What used to be called the eternal triangle. Although I do now detect the hint of a twist in its tail.'

'Well, that sounds promising. Proceed!'

'What we have here is that childless couple, who have been married for, let us say, ten or twelve years and who are now held together more by a shared interest in their work than by emotional ties. Then along comes an attractive and impressionable young woman from a more gracious and secure world and the inevitable happens. Not much, is it?'

'No, and I would have expected your celebrated imagination to have provided you with something a little more daring than that.'

'It has nothing to do with my imagination, it is a fact.'

'Oh, come on, Tessa! We've only been here for eight hours, all of which has been spent eating, or sleeping, or discussing our private affairs.'

'No, there was an hour in the middle when I was doing none of those things.'

'During which, I am to believe that Jake and Verity obligingly allowed you to stumble on them locked in each other's arms?'

'To be fair, I didn't actually see them, but they both told me in the clearest terms that they had been.'

'How very thoughtful!'

'It was forced on them. There hadn't been time to compare notes, with the result that the two accounts were somewhat different.'

'No wonder your curiosity was aroused! Tell me more!'

'I will, even though I'm aware that you're only humouring me. It may possibly have some bearing on your own problem.'

'I told you that had now been disposed of.'

'Yes, but it doesn't follow that it has become an unmentionable subject. When you've narrowly escaped being killed in a car crash, you're no longer afraid, once the danger has passed, but it doesn't usually make you reluctant to talk about it.'

'Stop arguing and go on with the story.'

'Well, you see, Robin, the period between lunch and tea is a very dead one at the hotel. The domestic staff disappears and the only residents, apart from ourselves, are an elderly couple, who are doubtless in the habit of taking an afternoon rest, having spent most of their lives in the tropics.'

'How did you pick up that information, if they were resting?'

'That's another story and it's not important. The point is that this afternoon was deader than most, in so far as Louisa had gone to Chissingfield. So, if Jake and Verity had wished to meet in the summer house, this was the moment for it.'

'Though not reckoning with you, of course?'

'Just so. When Verity left to come back to the house, having ostensibly been exercising the dog, she saw me on the terrace and instantly became far more out of breath and out of temper than was natural for a sporty, athletic type like her. Then, when she'd got herself together, she came and stood behind my chair, to find out whether I could see the summer house from where I was sitting.'

'And?'

'Finding that I could, she gave me a circumstantial account of how she had stopped off there, to pass the time of day with Jake, although she hadn't been able to stay for more than a minute.'

'And could you be sure that she had?'

' Jake saw to that. When it came to his turn, he said that he remembered having caught sight of Verity somewhere in the garden and had presumed she was taking Lupus for a walk.'

'Yes, well, that does sound highly incriminating, although, as you say, it's not exactly a novel situation and I doubt if it will provide enough interest to fill up the long days of leisure and pleasure that lie ahead. Perhaps you'll have better luck with the elderly couple from the tropics.

It might turn out that the suntan comes out of a bottle and that she isn't his wife at all, but the dispenser who concocted the untraceable poison from which his real wife died. If that fails, there's always Mr God and all the angels for you to work on. The barman says he's pretty often around, when in residence at his very gracious mansion.'

'Why does he say that? Is he American?'

'No, just getting into practice for the tourist season, I gather.'

'Well, thanks for the guidelines, which I am sure will come in handy, but I haven't quite finished with Jake yet, as it happens, and this is the bit which concerns you. You remember how I got it so fixed in my mind that this murder, which you are now able to talk about with such detachment, occurred four years ago, and not two?'

'What about it?'

'Well, it was Jake who fixed it there. And he didn't just throw it out in an absent-minded way, either. He said it was fixed in his own mind because it had coincided with him and Louisa taking over a pub in Chissingfield and that it had been a great help to them in building up a clientele in the bar. He was just as amateurish as Verity; not content with a slight deviation and leaving it there. He had to go and build it up with a lot of superfluous details.'

'I get your drift. You imply that he was lying about it deliberately, to confuse the issue, and therefore must have had some devious motive for doing so?'

'Why not?'

'But you also seem to be under the impression that half a dozen skilled and experienced men would have buzzed around asking questions and, having noted the answers, would take these as the final word on the subject. I assure you it is not so. Every single statement, however remotely connected with the case, was checked and cross-checked in a dozen different ways before being classified as reliable evidence. And, even supposing that despite all this, Jake had managed to put one over on us, what do you propose I should do about it now?'

'Oh, forget it, I suppose. I was rather pleased with myself for catching him out in a couple of whoppers in the space of ten minutes, but you've deflated me now.'

'Cheer up! As I say, the elderly couple are far more likely to provide you with some useful material to stave off the boredom. And if, by some misfortune, they should turn out to be exactly what they appear to be, we'll go to Bath tomorrow and try our luck at the theatre. They might even be doing one of those good old-fashioned plays which, unlike life, have a beginning, a middle and an end.'

(6)

'Here's one which fits the bill,' I said, having eased myself on to a bar stool and studied the brochure entitled "Forthcoming Attractions", which I had extracted from Verity. 'No loose ends here. All the misunderstandings sorted out and everyone back in his right place for the final curtain. Just as you like it, in fact.'

'Oh God, must we? Shakespeare's bad enough, but Shakespeare done by amateurs would be more than I could take.'

'These are not amateurs. It's a professional repertory company and they're here for a ten week season.

Furthermore, it says here that the theatre where they're playing is a converted Mill House of great charm and historical interest, set in the heart of the Mendip Hills, with its own bar and restaurant. How about that?'

'What else are they doing?'

'*The Doll's House* and a thriller, which was on last year in London. That won't do, you always say they're so untrue to life.'

'And so they are.'

'Which is what most people go to the theatre for.'

'Well, as long as they haven't transposed *As You Like It* to a prisoner-of-war camp, with an all-male cast, I suppose I could stand it. When is it?'

'Wednesday night and Thursday matinée, and I should imagine you'd be safe. So far as I can tell, the only innovation is that Jacques is played by a boy in his twenties, but I've no objection to that. I've heard young men pontificating just as often as elderly ones.'

I looked up at this point, to say good evening to an elderly one who had just entered the bar, accompanied by his wife. After the barest hesitation, they returned the greeting and sat down at a corner table. Mr Fellowes then called out for a large whisky and a dry sherry, though refraining, to my disappointment, from clapping his hands and addressing the barman as 'Boy'.

'Want to bet?' Robin asked, having glanced up and away from them again in the space of two seconds.

'If you like.'

'I'll lay a pound he's a retired bank manager, now following the advice which he hands out to so many of his pensioned customers and living in the Algarve.'

'You're on! I know for a fact that gin and tonic is the staple drink there. And I'll have another bet on the side.'

'What's that?'

'That we'll find out which of us is right before we go into dinner. Come on, I'm getting curvature of the spine, perched up here. Let's go and sit down comfortably.'

'Would you mind if we pinched your ashtray?' I asked, getting up again a few minutes later. 'I see you're not using it and there isn't one on our table.'

'Oh, please do! Delighted!' Mr Fellowes assured me, with old-world colonial charm, but his wife said in a drawly, amused voice:

'I think you'll find yours on the table behind you. I noticed you put it there before you sat down.'

'Did I really? How very stupid of me!'

Robin intervened at this point by saying: 'You must excuse Tessa. She would stoop to any gambit to enlarge her circle of friends.'

I considered this to be a graceful way of putting it and Mrs Fellowes evidently agreed, for she went one better: 'And it has saved us the trouble of inventing one of our own. Charles and I have been feeling so bored by the prospect of another evening with no one to talk to but each other.'

Mr Fellowes looked faintly startled to hear this, but Robin said:

'Then why don't we join you, but only on condition that I may order you both another drink!'

'Oh, very kind! Mine's a whisky and I expect Avril would like a dry sherry, wouldn't you, Avril?'

'I'm sure Mr Price knows that already, dear.'

'Tessa?'

'Not yet, thank you. This place is strangely deserted, isn't it? In view of its reputation, I'd have expected it to be packed out.'

'Oh well, Monday evening, you know, my dear. It will doubtless fill up as the week goes on. By Friday I daresay we shan't be able to move.'

'You're staying for the racing?'

'And beyond, I regret to say. It's not what one would have chosen, but we're likely to be here indefinitely, as far as I can see. Oh, thank you, Kenneth,' Mrs Fellowes added, as the barman arrived with their drinks. 'This is rather like the first night out, don't you think, Mrs Price? Here we are, complete strangers, drifting along in a timeless world, and by the end of the voyage we shall know all about each other and be swearing eternal friendship.'

'Never to meet again, I daresay,' Mr Fellowes remarked, sounding as though this was the best part, but I thoroughly approved of the simile, for it corresponded so well with the image I had created for her. I could just picture the stately P & O liner carving its majestic way through the Indian Ocean. And there was Mrs Fellowes, in a brocade evening dress, with a wisp of crimson gauze round her hair, to protect it from the salt breeze, emerging from her cabin on A deck, to dine at the Captain's Table.

'Not that I've ever been on a long sea voyage,' she added, 'but I was brought up on Somerset Maugham.'

'Avril's a great reader,' her husband explained.

'Yes, indeed! It is one of the few things which reconciles me to staying in hotels. How about you, Mrs Price? But perhaps you have to spend too much time reading your lines to have much time left over for books?'

'Tessa was brought up on Hollywood films,' Robin told her.

'Oh, lucky you! And are they what inspired you to become an actress?'

'Yes, I think they may have been.'

'And have you been to Hollywood yourself since then?'

'Only once.'

'Oh, but how fascinating! Do tell us about it! The cinema is another of my passions in life and I've always longed to see Hollywood. The nearest we ever got to it was Disneyland, which Charles adored, but I have to confess I found it rather boring. I don't suppose you ever met Cary Grant, by any chance?'

So there it was. Not unrewarding, naturally, and I reeled off a few well tried anecdotes which usually went down well, but whatever chance there had been of gathering information about the life and times of Mr and Mrs Fellowes had been snatched away. As Robin was quick to point out, when they left us to go into dinner.

'You would appear to have met your match there, Tessa. Round one to Mrs Fellowes, I think?'

'Yes, and that in itself was quite revealing,' I said, struggling to regroup my scattered forces.

'That's good! What did it reveal?'

'That she has something to hide. I now see them as a couple of smooth and high-powered crooks. I expect he acquired the suntan in Bermuda, where they have spent the past three weeks getting the cash laundered.'

'What makes you think so?'

'The accomplished way she fended off any questions about themselves. In my experience, most people welcome them, unless they have something to hide. The difficulty usually is to drag them away from the subject.'

'Well, perhaps bank managers' wives are exceptional in that way and, in any case, reticence doesn't necessarily imply something disgraceful. Shall we go and have dinner too? It may give you the strength to work out a new plan of attack.'

'No, I think I shall follow your example. I must try to remember that we are here to enjoy ourselves and not to go looking below the surface for things which don't concern us.'

When we stood up Kenneth came over to collect the glasses and Robin, who appeared to have become very chummy with him, although adopting the rather obsequious manner which men often use to people of that calling, remarked:

'Those are nice people we were talking to. Do they come here a lot?'

'Used to, not any more. Mr Fellowes retired a year or so ago and they went to live in the Caribbean. Virgin Islands, I guess it would be.'

'What did he do before he retired?' I asked, breaking the minute-old resolution.

'Estate agency, ma'am. His firm handled all the really big stuff in this area. His sons run the business now.'

Robin showed no more than a polite interest in this information, merely pointing out that I had lost one bet and won the other, but it made a deeper impression on me. During the short distance between the bar and the dining room I decided that perhaps after all I was not yet ready to devote myself exclusively to unwinding.

DAY TWO

(1)

THE next morning nothing had changed. The sun still shone and the sheep were still mooching about on the landscape in exactly the same formation as they had been the day before, and for the past decade, for all I knew. Even the knowledge that Mr Fellowes had once been a power in the estate agency world no longer inspired me. By the time we had finished breakfast, which Louisa had wheeled in on a trolley, and waded through every last word of two newspapers it was ten o'clock, which meant three hours to go before lunch.

So I engaged in my second battle with the crossword and then, when Robin had incarcerated himself in the bathroom, did what came naturally when faced with a crisis in my affairs, which was to pick up the telephone and dial my cousin Toby's number at Roakes Common.

It went on ringing for a minute and a half, but I was not deterred, for I knew it was too early for him to have gone out. It was more likely that he hoped, by ignoring it, to induce whoever was calling him to go away and leave him in peace. This proved to be correct and on about the sixtieth ring he lifted the receiver, saying:

'Is that you, Tessa?'

'How did you guess?'

'My sixth sense. What's the matter? Bored already?'

'Whatever gave you that idea?'

'My common sense. You don't mean something's happened?'

'No, nothing has happened, or is ever likely to. Now you mention it, I believe I am just the tiniest bit bored. If only I had some knitting it wouldn't be so bad. I think Robin is getting to that stage too, although nothing would make him admit it.'

'He doesn't know how to knit and neither do you.'

'We could learn. God knows, this is the moment for it. In fact, though, Toby, my real object in ringing is to tell you that you have been leaping up in my estimation.'

'Oh well, in that case, the holiday hasn't been entirely wasted. What, in particular, is so wonderful about me?'

'For all these years I've been deluding myself that your capacity for doing nothing for weeks on end sprang from laziness. I now see my mistake.'

'You call writing plays nothing?'

'Well, no, naturally not, but you must admit that you don't churn them out on a conveyor belt. Most of the time, they're just an excuse not to do anything else, which is where I underestimated you. I saw it as the easy way out, but I've now realised that it takes hard work and discipline.'

'Oh well, it hasn't always been easy, I admit, but I made up my mind early in life what I didn't want to do and I've tried to stick to it.'

'I wish I knew your secret.'

'I'll help you in any way I can. How would it be if I were to ask Mrs Parkes to send you a ball of wool and some needles?'

'Better than nothing, but it would take ages. What I'd really like is for you to bring them over yourself this afternoon.'

'My dear Tessa, have you gone mad? I thought it was the kind of foolhardy thing you have been praising me for not doing?'

' I know, but according to the AA book we're only eighty miles from Oxford, which means about the same from Roakes, and you wouldn't be bothered by the telephone once you were on the road. Also there isn't anything at all to do when you get here, so you won't even have to work at it. You'll be in your element.'

'I suppose, when you put it like that, it does sound rather tempting, but would they have a vacancy at such short notice?'

'They're packed out with vacancies. You can take your pick, with high-born girls to bring you tea in bed.'

'I realise that you would invent any old tale to get your own way, but isn't this rather a different tune from the one you were singing last week? I was given to understand that it was only through knowing people who were well placed in the Inns of Court that you were able to squeeze in at all.'

'That's what we though and perhaps it was true once. Not any more, though. It's like the grave now. A very comfortable, mink lined grave, I hasten to add. I don't know what's gone wrong, but there's hardly a customer in sight. They even conned Robin into signing on for three meals a day in advance, so do remember to ask for bed and breakfast only. On second thoughts, perhaps you'd like me to make the reservations for you?'

'I wouldn't particularly like it, but it might be preferable to staying here and being rung up every ten minutes.'

'Oh, thank you, Toby. I knew we could rely on you.'

'Who was on the telephone?' Robin asked.

'Toby.'

'Oh, really? What's he up to?'

'He's planning to join us for a day or two.'

'Is he, indeed? I thought he hated sleeping in strange beds?'

'He does, as a rule, but I painted it in such glowing colours that he couldn't resist coming to try it for himself. I hope I haven't overdone it.'

Due no doubt to some kindly intervention on the part of our guardian angel, there happened to be a vacant room on the same floor as ours, just across the passage, in fact.

'I'm afraid it doesn't have the view, though,' Louisa said, looking worried about it.

'Never mind, he can always come and feast himself on ours.'

'And he'll be arriving this evening? Jolly good! I take it he'll want full pension?'

'Well, no . . . that might be risky. He's on a diet, you see.'

'Not to worry. Just ask him to let us know what he can and can't eat and Jake will make sure it's specially prepared for him.'

'What service!' I said weakly.

'Oh well, we aim to please. Which reminds me, Tessa, I do hope you and Robin weren't kept awake by that radio blaring away last night?'

'What radio?'

'Someone left one switched on in the room next to yours. I didn't notice it until I brought your breakfast up. Rather mysterious, really, because Number Four isn't occupied at present, so I can't imagine what anyone was doing there in the first place. Still, not to worry, so long as it didn't disturb you. Is there anything else you need?'

'No, thanks. Except. . . . Is there a village within walking distance?'

'Mattingly Bottom is the nearest. A couple of miles, if you take the path through the fields. Not much to see when you get there, though.'

'No wool shop?'

'No, you'd have to go to Chissingfield for that.'

'Perhaps we'll try there this afternoon, but the first thing is to get an appetite for lunch, so we may as well start at the Bottom.'

After settling this business, I went out on to the terrace, where Robin, with his back to me, was talking to Mrs Fellowes, who was looking like exiled Royalty in her shell-pink silk dress and pearls.

'Not only distressing for you, but worrying too, I imagine,' I heard him say.

'Yes, you're so right, Mr Price. Very worrying, and boring as well, I'm afraid. Ah, and here is your wife! Is everything arranged, my dear? I hear that we are soon to have the opportunity of meeting the celebrated Toby Crichton? Things are looking up at Mattingly Grange.'

'You've heard of Toby?'

'But of course! Charles and I are great fans. Don't look so surprised.'

'It's just that, since you spend so much time abroad, I wouldn't have expected his name to mean anything to you.'

'We don't have the same opportunities for going to the theatre as we used to, it's true. That's the price we pay for all the year round sunshine, but when we're over here we try to pack in as many shows as we can, to make up for it. I sometimes think that we expatriates see more plays than you people who spend all your lives here.'

'Yes, I expect so. Like living in London and never setting foot in Westminster Abbey.'

'Yes, indeed! Well, you have a lovely morning for your walk, so I mustn't keep you. At least, let it not be said that you spent a whole week here without ever setting foot outside the hotel grounds.'

Accepting the dismissal, we took our leave and I said to Robin, as we walked down the steps to the lawn:

'How did she know we might stay for a whole week, when we've only booked in for two nights?'

'Been pumping the management, perhaps. As I warned you, you may have met your match in that one. I've a feeling there's a very shrewd brain ticking away behind the languid manner, and that she's mastered the trick of finding out all she needs to know, without giving much away in return. After all, what a splendid wife she would have made for a diplomat! Little does she know where her true vocation lay.'

'Although she does seem to have given something away to you. Why has she call to feel worried and distressed?'

'It was like a game of poker. I am afraid she has already discovered what my job is and she wanted some information from me, which she could only get by imparting some of her own.'

'What did she tell you?'

'Why they are here. They hadn't intended to come to England for another six weeks, when they would have moved back into their own house for the summer. It was on the outskirts of Chissingfield.'

'Was? Has it now moved somewhere else?'

'It was burnt down three weeks ago.'

'Oh, so that's why she doesn't know how long they'll be staying. How did it happen?'

'She didn't say, but evidently there's a whiff of arson in the air. She wanted my opinion as to how long it might take for the wheels to grind and the insurance company to pay up.'

'Were you able to tell her?'

'Of course not.'

'Well, at least in this case no suspicion could fall on the owners, since presumably they were in the Virgin Islands when it happened?'

'On the other hand, they have two grown up sons who were just round the corner when it happened.'

'But Kenneth told us they own the business now. If they wanted to raise money on the house all they had to do was to sell it at a somewhat inflated price, as only they would know how. They didn't have to burn it down.'

'It may not be so simple as that. She was very cagey, as I told you, but I did manage to glean a few facts and it appears that the house has been up for sale for over a year and no one has shown much interest, so it's obviously a bit of a white elephant.'

'It seems a curious mistake for a man in Mr Fellowes's position to have made. Saddling himself with a dud, when he could pick and choose.'

'Well, it had been their family home for thirty or forty years, but fashions have changed. It's a big, rambling, Victorian place, with no land to speak of. Just an acre or two, right on the edge of the town. That suited the Fellowes all right, but nowadays people who can afford a house of that size, with all the expense of keeping it up, want a lot of land to go with it. One way and another, the land has become more valuable than the buildings.'

'Honestly, Robin, you are well informed.'

'Well, that was the bait, of course. Taking me into her confidence, or pretending to, anyway.'

'But she didn't give you any details about the circumstances of this fire?'

'No, I had the feeling there was more to come, but then you appeared and she switched to the subject of Toby and his masterpieces.'

'I must contrive some more opportunities to throw you together. In the meantime, I don't suppose that Mr Fellowes's firm was the one Pauline worked for, by any chance?'

'No, they were called Winthrop Son and Gayford.'

'You remembered that, or did you look it up?'

'I checked it, but I had remembered. It had struck me as having a somewhat gentle and appealing ring about it, which one doesn't readily associate with that business. It wasn't so inappropriate as it sounded, though, because the Gayford half turned out to be a woman.'

'Husband and wife?'

'No, she'd originally been engaged by Winthrop senior as a shorthand typist, but he must have been ahead of his time, because he recognised her potential and encouraged her to rise in the world. He gave her time off to study and so on. By the time he died she'd become a fully fledged chartered surveyor and he'd made her a junior partner.'

'Good for him! And how about Pauline? Did she show signs of going the same way?'

'Not that I know of, although she was said to be exceptionally competent. She was Young Mr Winthrop's secretary. He was still known as Young Mr Winthrop, even though he was in his sixties and going deaf by then.'

Heartened by the way he described these matters, as though they belonged to fiction, instead of real life, I said:

'You never explained why Pauline was so set against racing?'

'No, and the answer is that it had killed her father, having first broken up his marriage. It left her, at the age of five, in the care of relatives, who did not underestimate the magnitude of their generosity in taking her in, or let a week go by without reminding her of it.'

'Yes, that sounds a pretty good reason, but could horses really be blamed for such a trail of disasters?'

'Her father was a National Hunt Jockey, which, as you know, can be a precarious way of earning a living. He was beginning to get established, though, and had just been taken on as stable jockey by quite a successful trainer, so things were looking up for him. Then came the accident.'

'A fall, you mean?'

'And no ordinary one. He was leading by two lengths when his horse stumbled and threw him at the last fence. It fell on top of him and the rest of the field, about twenty of them, came thundering up behind. He spent the next nine months in hospital, with multiple fractures in practically every bone in his anatomy.'

'It can happen.'

'Yes, but this was worse than most because his spine was affected. He was paralysed from the waist down.'

'Poor man!'

' Perhaps, in time, he would have recovered, but his wife didn't wait to find out. She ran off with another man. He was a jockey too and he'd been offered a well paid job in Hong Kong, which must have seemed like adding insult to injury. She also abandoned the child.'

'And he didn't recover?'

'He didn't wait to find out either. He shot himself.'

'How could he do that, if he was paralysed?'

'One afternoon they brought Pauline to visit him. They were left alone for ten minutes and he got her to climb on a chair and get his revolver out of a suitcase, which had been stacked on top of a cupboard. She and the nurse who'd been sent to fetch her and hand her over to the uncle and aunt were only halfway down the corridor when they heard the shot. It put her off horses for good.'

'The wonder is that she should have chosen to spend her life in Chissingfield, where you can hardly avoid them.'

'It's not unique in that. You'd have your work cut out to find a town in the south of England which isn't within reach of a race course. Besides, her adoptive parents were living in Taunton when she went to them and she was at school and college there. They were her only means of support, so there was no possibility of breaking away until she was qualified to earn her living. After that, she naturally didn't want to move to a strange neighbourhood where she had no friends or connections. Also, despite everything, she seems to have felt some affection for her uncle and aunt, who were getting on in years and may have mellowed a bit by then. When she got the job with Winthrop and Gayford she moved into lodgings in the town, but once every two or three months she took the bus to Taunton and spent Sunday, or sometimes the whole weekend, in what, after all, was the only home she could remember.'

'How long had this been going on when she was killed?'

'Three or four years. Then her uncle died and her aunt sold up and went to live in a bungalow in Worthing. So the regular visits came to an end, but Pauline still kept in touch and made a point of going to see her once or twice a year.'

'So when her home had gone, what charms did Chissingfield hold for her, apart from her job?'

'Everything she needed, apparently. She was country born and bred and there's no shortage of green pastures around here, as you know so well. She seems to have been a reserved sort of girl, without strong emotional entanglements, but she had friends here, people she'd known since her schooldays and new ones she'd met at the office. And you have to remember that, although they hold about ten meetings a year, the race course is several miles from the town and doesn't impinge on it to any great extent. We discovered people who'd spent half their lives here and never set foot on the race course.'

'And Pauline was one of them?'

'She never went herself, but it didn't seem to have bothered her that other people did. Except, that is, on one special day of the year and thereby hangs the rest of the tale. Perhaps we should shelve that for the time being, though, since we now seem to be faced with a decision of some gravity.'

I could see what he meant. Our footpath had been ascending sharply for the last quarter of a mile and had now brought us to a stile, which separated it from a narrow road on the outskirts of the village. There were one or two medium sized, newish looking houses on this level, but not for nothing had it been named Mattingly Bottom. Fifty yards from where we stood the road curved round to the right and began a steep and winding descent to a huddle of buildings crammed into a hollow.

Louisa's warning that it had little to offer when you got there, and the inescapable truth that whoever walked down must walk up again, naturally prompted us to turn back. The only reason to waver was a signpost on the left-hand side of the road, at the point where the right-hand side disappeared from view. We were too far off to decipher the words, but the oak leaf design, inviting us to set our feet in the direction of some historic treasure trove, was hard to resist. Dedicated holidaymakers, as we had set out to be, we had not neglected to bring our National Trust cards, so it was not even going to cost us anything.

'Tell you what,' Robin said, 'we'll compromise. It's now five to eleven. If we haven't caught sight of whatever it is when the hour strikes, we'll turn back. What do you say?'

We stretched it a bit, needless to say, but still the effort was wasted. The hands stood at three minutes past eleven when we saw our second oak leaf, this one beckoning us down a leafy lane, which stretched away in a dead straight line to infinity.

'What we could do now,' I said, 'is to make another compromise. Give it up and come back in the car this afternoon. We might even find out first whether the damn thing is open on Tuesdays.'

Robin was not listening. His attention had now strayed to a house on our left, diagonally opposite the turning to the lane. It was larger and older looking than any we had so far passed, but otherwise unremarkable, except in one particular. There was a notice board nailed to the front gate, announcing that its sale was under offer and that the agents who were handling it were called Fellowes and Gayford.

'What does that mean?' I asked.

'The two firms have amalgamated, presumably. Or, to put it another way, the big fish has gobbled up the little one. Come on, let's go back now, shall we, and live to fight another day?'

'I worry about Young Mr Winthrop,' I said, as we plod-ded up the winding hill. 'I do hope the big fish hasn't spat him out. I had begun to feel quite attached to him.'

'Now, don't start getting maudlin, Tessa. That would be the last straw.'

'It's your fault. Transporting oneself back into the past, for whatever reason, is bound to bring trouble. If you'd told me from the beginning what lay behind this so-called holi-day, I could have warned you about some of the pitfalls.'

'Although I can't say you've worked very hard since then to protect me from them. All you do is keep asking questions and pitchforking me into more of them. It will be quite a relief when Toby is here and we can talk about something else.'

'Don't depend on it,' I said, cheered by the sight of the stile and the knowledge that it would soon be downhill all the way. 'You know as well as I do that he likes nothing belter than to sit back and let someone else work out a plot for him. So far as I know, he's never used the cut and thrust of an estate agents' office as a setting for a play, but I daresay he'll find possibilities in it, so be on your guard.'

(3)

Lupus was not in the reception hall when Toby arrived, nor Verity either, which was not such good news, and it was only by chance that I saw his car from the bedroom window, while changing for dinner.

Ten minutes went by, still with no word or sound from Number Four, so I put on my dressing gown, hoping it would pass for an evening cloak, and went downstairs to see what had become of him. He was seated in one of the chintzy armchairs, reading a local paper.

'How long have you been here?' I asked him.

'About an hour.'

'Oh no, Toby, that must be an exaggeration.'

'Possibly. So far as I am concerned, time has now stood still.'

'Well, never mind, you will get used to that and it is one of the charms of this place. So happy-go-lucky, you know, and you are free to come and go as you please.'

'So I should hope, since I see it is advertised in this paper as a hotel and not a prison.'

'All I meant was that you don't have to bother with formalities, like signing the register and so on. It so happens that I know exactly where they've put you and, if you will follow me, I will conduct you to your room.'

I lifted the flap and went behind the reception desk, taking down the key of Number Four from its hook and then, hearing the front door open, twirled round with a guilty start, to be greeted by a familiar tenor voice:

'Oh no, I don't believe it! I positively do not believe it. And Toby too, I do declare! Have you taken the place over? Well, high time somebody did and I can't think of two nicer people.'

He was an actor named James Featherstone, the very one, in fact, whose name I had noticed in the cast list of *As You Like It*, although I had exaggerated a little in describing him as a boy in his twenties. It would be more accurate to say that he was a boy in his thirties. Although it was some years since we had met, at one point, when we had played opposite each other as a couple of moony teenagers in a television serial, we had become as intimate as his nature would allow. This was not saying much because, although a celebrated chatterbox, he had few close friends. So far as I could remember, the nearest he had come to confiding in me was in confessing that Featherstone was his mother's maiden name and that he had chosen it partly because it looked better on the credits, but principally to dissociate himself from his detestable father.

'Oh, hallo Jimmie!' I said. 'How are you?'

'Very well, thank you, darling. How's Price?'

Not many people in my circle refer to Robin as Price, but Jimmie always made a point of doing so. His explanation was that Robin was an unsuitable name for one engaged in such sinister activities, but I suspected that it might have had more to do with the fact that it so closely resembled the name of his own beloved companion. Reminded of this, I said:

'He's very well too. How's Bobbie?'

'Splendid, thank you.'

'And what brings you here, if one may ask a personal question?'

'No, one may not. I hate having my line pinched and I consider I have far more right to this one. Furthermore, I have to say that I am not sure you will get very far in this new venture of yours, if this is the style in which you intend to greet all your customers. It might have been more *comme il faut* to have climbed out of your negligee by seven-thirty in the evening. Unless, of course, you hope to attract a more raffish type of clientèle than the tweedy lot one is accustomed to seeing here. In which case, you are probably going the right way about it.'

'What I'm doing,' I explained, 'is finding the key to Toby's room. And the reason for my question is that I was under the impression that you were even now on your way to another part of the forest, in order to give out the news that all the world's a stage and all the men and women merely players.'

'Tomorrow at this time I shall be doing just that. Tonight they are in another part of Norway, which is no concern of mine, thank God. I have been summoned here by my father,

whose birthday it is, to celebrate the dawn of another nefari-
ous year in his life.'

'Oh, I see! And, since it might get the festivities off to a
better start if I were not parading about in my negligee when
he arrives, we shall leave you to it. See you later, maybe.'

Verity came marching through from the lounge, as
we were halfway up the stairs, so I leaned over the banis-
ter to introduce her to Toby and explain about the key.
She responded with a certain degree of head-tossing and
outraged amazement, but it soon fizzled out. Almost immediately she caught sight of Jimmie and her expression changed
to one of goggle-eyed astonishment. She stared at him, with
her mouth hanging open and looking as though she were
about to burst into tears.

This reaction, although somewhat overcharged, came
as no great surprise, for I had seen him provoke a similar
one in adoring women who had waited for hours in the
pouring rain, with their autograph books at the ready. I
could have warned her, however, that, so far as they and
she were concerned, signing autographs was where it would
begin and end.

He had fallen in love many years ago with a woman
fifteen years older than himself and had remained so ever
since. Her name was Roberta Grayle and she was married
to a writer and reformed alcoholic, whom she watched over
like a female dragon guarding its young. Believing that without her, Max would inevitably revert to his bad old ways,
she had refused to leave him and, by way of compromise,
Jimmie had moved in with them, to become a permanent
member of the household and part-time guardian.

So far as I knew, from that day forward he had never
seriously glanced at another woman and I had always
believed this state of affairs to be at the root of the hostil-
ity between him and his family. However, he was reticent

to the point of secrecy on this, as on most subjects which concerned him personally and, curious as ever about other people's lives, I welcomed this chance to see and possibly meet his father and to discover more about their relationship.

(4)

'And while you were downstairs seeing to the running of the hotel,' Robin said, 'I have had a visitor. Honestly, I don't see how you can be bored. One can never tell from one minute to the next 'what they are going to spring on you.'

'Who was your visitor? Lupus?'

'No, Louisa.'

'But how can that be? Did she fly in on a broomstick, or had she been lurking in the bathroom?'

'No, just the usual, conventional means of entry.'

'But Toby and I were in full view of the staircase and we didn't see her.'

'It seems to have escaped your notice, but there is a back staircase at the end of this passage, leading to a garden door and the kitchen, where the current crisis is now raging.'

'What's happened? Creosote in the soup?'

'Worse! She did her best to make light of it, but she was seething with rage behind the smiles. Apparently, the oil pipe to the stove has got blocked up and it's not functioning. It must have started cooling down some time in the afternoon, but no one noticed it until after six, by which time it was too late to get anyone to come and fix it.'

'What does that mean? Cold dinner?'

'They might have got away with that, if it had just been ourselves and the Fellowes to cater for, but there's a gala on tonight. A birthday party, with a dozen guests, and the booking was made weeks ago. They've got an electric stove for emergencies, but it's barely adequate for a fiesta of this kind, so they want us to take it in shifts. Louisa came to ask if we'd mind very much holding back till eight forty-five or nine.'

'I do mind, as it happens, because all that exercise has sharpened my appetite, but I suppose it can't be helped. What did you say?'

'Oh, I agreed. It seemed more sensible to make a virtue of necessity than to insist on our rights. Nothing could be more dispiriting than sitting round a bare table, watching other people have a hilarious time at their groaning board. I went so far as to say we shouldn't even enjoy being in earshot of the hilarity and groans and would have our drinks served up here this evening.'

'Do we fetch them ourselves?'

'No, it's all organised. We ring reception when we're ready and Verity will transmit the order to Kenneth.'

'I'm ready now, so start ringing.'

There was no reply from reception, so he said he would give it another five minutes and then try again. Ten minutes later he went down to fetch the drinks himself.

'You do see what I mean?' I asked Toby, who had just walked in. 'If we were at home now we could simply cross the floor and pour out whatever we wanted to drink and have dinner at whatever time we wanted to eat. It does seem absurd to dole out huge sums of money just to be denied such basic rights.'

'And it's not as though either of you was housebound. So far as I understand the position, you are both condemned to spending the greater part of your lives in uncomfortable or uncongenial surroundings, so why you should torture yourselves in this way is something of a mystery.'

'It's all bound up with Robin's *recherche du temps perdu*. Some case he worked on down here a year or two ago, which was never solved and which he's been having nightmares about ever since. This is supposed to get it out of his system, but it doesn't seem to be succeeding.'

'I can see how it would worry him, although personally I have a sneaking admiration, or fellow feeling, for the criminals who get away with it.'

'Then you had better get him to tell you about it. I was hoping you would. The sooner we get him sorted out, the sooner we can pack our bags and go home. I'll just give you the broad outline.'

'All's well,' Robin said, 'Kenneth has laid on everything we're likely to need to keep us going for an hour or so. And guess who the birthday boy is? Two lumps of ice if you get it right.'

'It wouldn't be fair, because I know already. Unless there are two of them, it's Jimmie Featherstone's father.'

'Perhaps there are two, then. Mine is called Godstow.'

'Oh, really? Well, that would explain why he's always been so cagey about his family. I bet he's as relieved as we are that we're not in the dining room, watching every move and taking notes. Anyway, why don't we while away the time by telling Toby about Pauline? He thinks it might give him ideas for a play.'

'Yes, indeed!' my cousin said, coming up to scratch for once. 'And I have to say I'm agog. Tessa tells me that ten days went by before anyone noticed that she wasn't around and that it can all be explained by the fact that she didn't care for racing. I'm not demented about it myself, but I hadn't realised what it could lead to.'

'Then you wouldn't know anything about the February National Hunt meeting at Chissingfield?'

'No, I wouldn't.'

'In these parts it's the most important event in the racing calendar. The big race, which is called the Mortimer Handicap, after the brewers who sponsor it, carries a prize of twenty thousand and it's also a sort of run-up to the Grand National. So it attracts all sorts of people who don't normally bother to come here, and all sorts of interest on and off the course. For those two days Chissingfield is on the map and the whole town benefits. However, the Mortimer Handicap happens to be the race in which Pauline's father had the accident which led to his death. As a result, she always took that week off from work, as part of her annual holiday.'

'But surely the point of that would have been to get as far from the scene as possible?' Toby said. 'Not, one would have thought, to go for moonlight walks beside the race course? Or are we to believe that it had a morbid fascination for her?'

'On the contrary, she always did go away. Abroad, if she could manage it, and for the whole week, not returning until Sunday, after the crowds had left and things were back to normal. Only that year there was a break in the pattern. Her aunt had been ill and Pauline had offered to give up part of her holiday to go and stay with her. She wasn't prepared to sacrifice all of it, however, and was to spend the first three or four days redecorating her bedsitter and go to Worthing from Thursday to Sunday. According to her landlady and other witnesses who saw her at the time, the first three days went exactly according to plan but she never got to Worthing.'

'But didn't the aunt make a few enquiries when she failed to turn up?'

'No. On Thursday afternoon, when tea was on the table, she received a telegram. It had been sent from Chissingfield at twelve forty-eight and was read out to her over the telephone, those being the days when such things were possible. The operator asked her if she wanted a copy through the post and she replied that she did not. The message was quite unambiguous. Due to an unavoidable change of plans, Pauline was unable to come. She sent her love and would be writing. To have had it confirmed would only have rubbed salt in the wound.'

'And there was quite a wound to rub it in, presumably?'

'She told us she was bitterly disappointed, but according to one of the few neighbours with whom she was on speaking terms, her principal reaction was anger and self-pity. She became more enraged than ever when no letter arrived, but it never occurred to her to doubt that Pauline had sent the telegram herself, or that there was any cause for worry. She simply assumed that the ungrateful hussy had found a more amusing way to spend her holiday.'

'But, Robin, when you first started on this story, which seems such ages ago now, you told me that she had been killed at around midnight on Thursday, so how did she spend the hours between not going to Worthing and getting herself killed?'

'If anyone could have given us the answer to that one, there's a good chance I should never have been called in at all, and we shouldn't be here now, but those ten or eleven hours have never been accounted for. She walked out, carrying a suitcase, just after one o'clock on Thursday, having said goodbye to her landlady and reminding her that she would be back on Sunday. That was the last anyone saw of her. It was ten minutes' walk to the station and there's a fast train to Paddington at one twenty-five, so presumably that's the one she caught, or set out to catch, always providing, of course, that the telegram had been sent to her aunt without her knowledge.'

'Weren't you able to trace it?'

'It had been handed in over the counter at her sub-post office. It was the lunch hour, which is always a busy time, and the clerk couldn't remember much about the sender, except that it was a young woman, so it could well have been Pauline. She didn't possess a private telephone and, although her landlady had one, she didn't encourage her lodgers to use it, except for emergencies. There is also the possibility that Pauline didn't want anyone to know about her change of plans and wasn't going to risk being overheard.'

'I can understand how tiresome and frustrating it must have been for you,' Toby said, 'but whether she meant to go to Worthing or not, she seems to have gone out of her way to emphasise that she would return on Sunday, and what I cannot understand is why no one noticed it when she failed to turn up, either then or at her place of work on Monday.'

'Then you must blame Tessa. She obviously hasn't explained what we were up against with Mother Nature.'

'He means the weather,' I said, doing so now.

'Yes, you did tell me how it gummed things up for Robin, but since no one knew that she was dead, I still can't understand why her absence caused no comment.'

'Because such absences became the rule during the whole of that week and part of the following one. It was no ordinary cold snap, I should explain. Conditions were worse than at any time since the records began and no one, particularly in this part of England, where they are used to comparatively mild winters, was prepared for it, or had the resources to cope. Hundreds of trains had to be cancelled and hundreds of roads became impassable again within hours of being cleared. Every day about half the people employed in Chissingfield either couldn't get to work at all, or straggled in hours late; and you may be sure that a few others made it the excuse to do just that. In fact, Young Mr Winthrop may have been one of them, although one assumes that his was a genuine case, since, as head of the firm by then, he had most to lose by allowing the office to run itself without him.'

'Meaning that he didn't turn up for work either?'

'Not during the first week. His wasn't a transport problem because he lived right in the town, but he'd had bronchitis not so long before and his doctor had advised him to stop indoors. People took the attitude that Pauline would have got there, if it had been humanly possible, but there was no special surprise, certainly no anxiety, when she didn't. It was a situation for any murderer to dream about and to say that the trail was cold by the time we got to it would be to repeat a pun which came dangerously near to causing several other murders around that time.'

'So it is hard to see why you ever expected to catch him, or should be torturing yourself years later because you didn't.'

'Vanity, I suppose, combined with an ingrained dislike of unfinished business. Still, between you, you've shaken me out of it and we needn't let it spoil things any more. On the whole, I'd prefer you not to try and base a play on it either. As Tessa knows so well, I'm old-fashioned and I like them to have a beginning, a middle and an end.'

'Then I must try to invent an ending for you and, if I succeed, it may come true. As Tessa also knows, life may he stranger than fiction, but it also has a way of imitating it.'

(5)

The birthday party was still in semi, if not full, swing in the dining room, although presenting a rather more sombre face to the world than is generally associated with such occasions. There were a dozen people seated round the centre table, seven of whom were known to us. These were Mr Godstow and his son and daughter, whose resemblance to each other accounted for my impression of having seen her before, Diana's giggly friend Stephanie, Jock Symington and Mr and Mrs Fellowes.

Outstanding among the unknowns was a raven-haired, hawk-faced woman, with wine-red nails, sea-green eye shadow and tinted spectacles, seated on the right of her host. However, there was no time to play the game of inventing her history and background because Robin forestalled me by providing us with the real one.

'You remember my telling you that the Furies were gathering?' he asked in a low voice, as we all pretended to study the menu. 'The witch in the place of honour is Irene Gayford. All we need now to make it a full house is Young Mr Winthrop.'

'Stop mumbling and speak up, please!' Toby said. 'The author is entitled to some rights, you know.'

This was not the moment to observe them, however, for our arrival had not passed unnoticed and a hum of semi-audible mutterings could be heard from the big table, with Jimmie's tenor voice taking the solo part. So I picked up a card headed *Cuisine Minceur* which had been thoughtfully provided and on the back of it wrote down the names of six of the supporting cast.

'You have introduced two new characters,' he complained. 'I am not sure I need them at this stage.'

'They are not new to us, but we hadn't realised they were Furies.'

'And I must try to keep my paranoia within bounds,' Robin said. 'After all, it is only to be expected that the Fellowes should know these people and there is no reason to suppose that the party has been arranged specially to torment me.'

He was able to make these comments in a relatively normal tone, because the members of the birthday party were now standing up, preparatory to withdrawing. Jimmie detached himself and came over to join us.

'I bring bad news,' he said, seating himself between Robin and Toby.

'I hope you haven't come to tell us that the electric stove has broken down?'

'Not so far as I know, darling. This is a message from my father. I am ashamed to say that he didn't recognise you, Tessa, but now that he knows who you are . . .'

'And he would need to be deaf, if he didn't, since I heard you repeating my name no less than three times.'

'Now that I've got it through to him who you are, he is suitably impressed and I am to convey his compliments and inform you that he would be honoured if you and your companions would take a liqueur with him in the bar when you have finished your dinner. Do not be deceived by the old world courtesy. It is merely an affectation to conceal the thug within.'

'Very kind, nonetheless, and I am sorry that we must decline,' Robin said firmly. 'As no one has taken our order yet, there appears to be small prospect of finishing our dinner before midnight.'

'No matter. The party is unlikely to break up until the small hours, however much the guests may suffer. Like so many successful criminals, he requires very little sleep and likes to be entertained during the waking hours. In any case, I'm afraid your lovely excuse is about to be torn from you,' Jimmie added, looking across the room at Louisa, who was now pushing her way through the tables towards us, in the preoccupied manner of one rehearsing her lines:

'Sorry about this, chaps!' she announced, forcing them out with a jollity born of desperation. 'Slight crisis in the kitchen. Chef wants to know if you'd mind putting up with some cold consommé and some ham and salad, just this once? It's home-made consommé, let me assure you, and we lay on a special salad dressing without oil.' She added, casting a look at Toby, 'There'll be an adjustment on the bill, naturally.'

We accepted our fate and when she had gone Toby said:

'To think I might be sitting at my own table at this moment, being looked after and looked up to by Mrs Parkes, who, with all her faults, does not realise that cold ham is fit for human consumption and neither knows nor cares how to make a salad dressing without oil. If this is what they call Home from Home, I can only say that the average home leaves a lot to be desired.'

'I entirely agree with you,' Jimmie said. 'I have always considered the place to be dreadfully over-rated, but be careful not to say so in the presence of my father. Something tells me he has sunk what he would call a tidy sum in it and, since sunk is likely to be the *mot juste*, it is a sensitive area. Although, when I say a tidy sum, I should explain that it is one which would mean absolutely nothing to him, unless he was in danger of losing it, at which point it becomes more precious than his life's blood.'

He was obliged to pause and draw breath here because the waitress had arrived with our cold collation and some confusion then arose because Robin had omitted to order the wine and the list did not appear to be immediately available. Jimmie finally solved the problem by pointing out that there were still two unopened bottles of birthday champagne languishing in the ice bucket and by commanding our servitor in a Crown Princely fashion to bring them over. This done, he took the floor again:

'Yes, it really is the only way I can account for his spending so much time here and using it for ghastly occasions like tonight. He probably deludes himself that it is a good advertisement and also that his mere presence keeps them all on their toes, whereas, of course, it has precisely the opposite effect, throwing them into transports of panic-stricken inefficiency. What intrigues me, though, if I may make so bold, is what brings you three here? It is definitely not the kind of place, even on its good days, which I associate with sophisticates like yourselves.'

'Which is one reason for choosing it,' I explained. 'We are here to get away from all that. Also, and mainly, of course, for the racing.'

'Oh, is that all? How tame! Somehow, I got the idea there was something more sinister behind it. Anyway, my father will be relieved.'

'What possible difference could it make to him?' Robin asked.

'Oh well, you see, once I'd got it through to him who Tessa was, his next question, naturally, was to know what you did for a living and when I told him he was shaken to the core. I was quite afraid he would stand up and croak "It's a fair cop, Guv."'

'Why? What's he done?'

'Plenty in his time, you may be sure. For all I know, there isn't a widow or orphan in the country who doesn't start the day by cursing him, but that's not the point. So many rich people are martyrs to the guilt complex, don't you find? Making money comes so dead easy to them that they're always expecting to be found out. It makes them more vulnerable than the rest of us, who soldier on, trusting to luck that we shan't be found out, which is one reason why I refused to follow in his footsteps. I thought I'd be on a safer wicket learning to talk posh and earn my living the hard way.'

'And you're not afraid of being found out in that?'

'No, Price, dear, I don't make enough money out of it for anyone to bother. Just look at me now, plodding through this crummy season at the Old and horrible Mill. However, being related to the old gangster does occasionally have its uses and here is a little something for your darling wife. Don't forget, Tessa, that if he should happen to mention some shares which might be worth investing a bob or two, you should telephone your stockbroker first thing in the morning. He only ever gives advice to pretty women, or people he wants to curry favour with, and he's always right, so you'll be playing on an easy wicket this evening.'

'Thank you, Jimmie, I'll do my best to keep a straight bat.'

'And here's some more advice, while I'm in this expansive mood, although this is by way of being a warning from the captain. If Jock Symington sends you down a ball called hot tip for the big race, don't be tempted. He's always wrong.'

(6)

'Oh yes, indeed!' I said, doing my best to look like a pretty woman. 'We're old friends. Many's the time he's saved my sanity when we've been kept hanging around on the set for hours. And of course we share a keen interest in cricket.'

' That so? Well, you live and learn in this world, don't you?'

'It's like the Church, you know. Very much part of the theatrical tradition.'

'Is it now? Still, I can't quite picture a young lady like yourself bowling overarm.'

'No, I'm only a spectator, I never got beyond batting with the wrong end of a tennis racquet, but Jimmie's a demon with the slow, left arm spin, you know.'

'Yes, I've heard he takes part in these charity matches and so forth. Nothing wrong with that, I daresay . . . good publicity too, but I've never taken much interest in cricket myself. Soccer now, that's different. That's always been my game.'

'Oh, how nice!' I said, wishing that Jimmie had remembered to prime me about this too. 'Do you do the pools?'

'Used to, in my younger days. Don't get time for gambling now. Don't approve of it, either.'

'But you do bet on horses?'

'No, never.'

'Really? On principle?'

'It doesn't appeal to me. It's the breeding and blood-stock side of racing which interests me, plus all the skill and know-how which goes into bringing a horse up to its best, when that's what you need from it. Prize money now, that's something else. I've no objection to that. It's the reward which comes from a combination which I'd call ninety per cent knowledge and ten per cent luck. Fair enough, in my opinion, but for the punters it's the other way on. More like ninety per cent luck and no one should expect to be given that more than once or twice in a lifetime.'

'Will you have any horses running at Chissingfield this week?'

'Two. One on Friday, one Saturday.'

'But you wouldn't advise me to back them?'

'No, and if you find that inconsistent, I'll explain. I may believe that I know all I need to know about my own horses, and they wouldn't be entered if they weren't intended to win, but what do I know about the other runners in those two races? Not enough is the answer. No way of being sure that one of them can't produce that extra burst of speed or stamina to outdo mine. That's a chance I'm willing to take, but I wouldn't risk money on it and I wouldn't advise anyone else to.'

I regarded this homily as the ideal introduction to some advice about another form of investment which he would recommend someone to put their money into, but he let it go by and I said:

'Were you here two years ago, when they had that murder at Chissingfield?'

Mr God looked across the room at Robin before he spoke, but his answer contained no reference to him, nor much to the question either:

'I have good reason to remember that meeting. Not because of the murder, we didn't hear about that until weeks later, but it was a classic example of the point I've just been making.'

'In what way?'

'I had a horse running on the opening day. It had marvellous form and the going was just right. We didn't think anything could beat him and no one else did either. He started at four to five on. When it came to the race he went over every jump like a bird and then right at the end he just gave up. Nothing wrong with him, he was as fit as a fiddle when he came into the ring, but he somehow seemed to lose interest. Beaten by his stable companion, too. Funny creatures, horses.'

'Very disappointing for you, but doesn't it rather contradict your theory?'

'Not a bit of it. Confirms it. Everything was right, except for that one unknown factor, which at the end of the day was what counted.'

'Then I must be stupid, because I was under the impression that the unknown factor came from ignorance about the rival horses. Surely, if these two were from the same stable, your trainer must have known them both equally well? So why didn't he realise that this was liable to happen? Or is the luck element after all more powerful than you care to admit?'

'Good question, young lady, and I must remember to pass it on to Jock some time,' Mr God remarked reflectively, tapping half an inch of ash from his cigar.

I could scarcely believe that he had failed to do so, either at the time, or at regular intervals ever since, but it was no part of my plan to create animosity, while the chance of hot tips on the stock exchange hung in the balance, so to steer the boat into smoother waters, I said:

'Do you read crime stories?'

'Can't say I do. Enough of it about, without turning to fiction. What made you ask?'

'I was reminded of something my cousin said this evening. How fiction can often be one jump ahead of fact and I believe it may apply particularly to crime stories.'

'Perhaps because they make popular reading among criminals, gives them ideas? What reminded you, though? Been reading one of those yarns about bent jockeys and crooked trainers?'

'No, but one might have supposed that only in a novel would you be likely to find a gathering of more than a dozen people, some of them strangers to each other, but nearly all with some particular reason to remember an event which took place over two years ago. Yet here we are, in real life, you see, in exactly that situation. Don't you find that weird?'

'Up to a point, but I'm not over impressed. Coincidence has played its part in my life more often than luck. And when you look at it you'll realise that it has only played a small part tonight. It's really confined to the single fact that you happen to know my son. The rest of us are either friends or business acquaintances from way back, and frankly I doubt whether that particular event you mentioned affected any of them very much. In fact, my dear young lady, the only person for whom it did have any special importance is your husband, who I understand was in charge of the case?'

'Who told you that?'

'Irene. I forget how it came up, but it seems she recognised him as soon as you came into dinner tonight. Met Irene Gayford, have you? She's the one talking to your husband now. Having a good natter about old times, I daresay.'

It was not something I would have dared to say myself, because Robin, although conducting himself in a reasonably civilised way, to the initiated eye was displaying unmistakable signs of boredom and fatigue. However, I was not quite ready to leave yet and returning my attention to Mr God, I said:

'Which category is she in? Friend or business acquaintance?'

'Irene? Bit of both, you could say.'

'And why would Robin have met her when he was here before?'

'She was the girl's employer.'

'Oh, I see! So, after all, it would have a special importance for her, presumably? Did she have any theories about who the murderer was?'

'Expect so, although I can't remember what they were. People round here were talking about nothing else for weeks afterwards and theories were two a penny in those days. Perhaps your husband has been asking her the same question.'

'I doubt it. He's been switched to another department now and that case would no longer concern him, even if it were still open.'

'So this is just a holiday, is it?'

'For me it is, but I'm not so sure about Robin. Perhaps I ought not to say this, although it's not really giving anything away because he never tells me anything that I couldn't read in the papers, but I have a feeling this may be one of those times when he's throwing in a little business with the pleasure.'

'That so? Funny it should have brought him back to Chissingfield?'

'Not really. This new job takes him all over the place.'

'What sort of thing does it involve, then?'

'All sorts. Racketeering, arms and drug smuggling, mainly; and some of the people he's trying to track down have their headquarters in places you'd never associate with crime on the grand scale.'

'Well, it's nice to know we've got chaps like him beavering away on our behalf. And now, have you time for another brandy, or are you one of the early birds?'

There was only one polite answer to that, so I gave it, then rounded up the rest of our party and said goodnight.

Jimmie accompanied us as far as the hall and, when I had arranged with him for three tickets to be left at the box office on the following evening, I said:

'It would be depressing to believe that I'm not pretty enough, so I must conclude that your father is not so eager to placate Robin as you supposed, since I have nothing to tell my stockbroker tomorrow.'

'Yes, something has thrown him, I can tell. You seemed to be doing so well, but then I noticed that expression on his face which I have learnt to associate with the bottom falling out of the mustard market, or some such catastrophe. God knows what you've been saying to him, but the trouble with you, Tessa is that, once started, you're all too liable to get carried away.'

(7)

'The only explanation that springs to mind,' I said, when Robin and I were back in the cocoon of Numbers Two and Three, 'is that I took the liberty of hinting that you were on the track of some big-time operators in the smuggling racket.'

'And a most diabolical one, I may say. Whatever possessed you?'

'It had dawned on me that nobody, however much you protested, was prepared to believe in your claim to be here as a private unwinder. I am afraid that is the effect the word 'police' has on people. It creates a malaise and brings out all their guilt feelings and they simply cannot accept the fact that a policeman is ever off duty. I daresay they are right not to, but the sad fact is that he has only to set foot in some pub, for instance, for all present to assume that he has done so for the sole purpose of making sure the landlord isn't giving short measure, or bending the licensing laws.'

'I know all that and I'm not denying it. It was my bad luck that Jake should have recognised me and spread the news to everyone within earshot, but I still can't see how you expect the situation to be improved by putting it around that I'm looking for smugglers.'

'Well, don't you see, Robin, it's one of those crimes which the vast majority have neither committed, nor been tempted to. Most people have done their share of cheating and fiddling at some point along the way, but high powered racketeers are a million miles out of that league. So once they know that's where your interest lies, they relax. They can look you in the eye and stop behaving like guilty school-boys. That was what I had in mind, but the annoying thing is that I may have misjudged the situation. I was slightly unnerved by Jimmie's parting remark about his father, because I'd noticed it too.'

'Noticed what too?'

'That he was quite loquacious and at ease when the subject of Pauline's murder came up, but as soon as I started babbling on about this new job of yours, the wind veered to the north east. So the conclusion I draw from that is that he's mixed up in some shady financial deal, is now afraid that you're on to him and is in a great hurry to cover his tracks and send out directives to the accomplices to lie low for a bit.'

'Yes, it would be, of course. It would never occur to you, for example, that he was feeling tired after a long hard birthday and wished to spend what remained of it tucked up in bed?'

'No, because Jimmie told us the party would go on till the small hours. Obviously, his father is one of those frenetic people who can manage with three hours' sleep, when all about them are dropping with fatigue. People who can get through an evening like that on tonic water must have twenty times the average stamina.'

'On the other hand, if he were involved in something fishy, wouldn't it have been more natural to try and draw you out, instead of snubbing you?'

'He's too wily for that. I'd already made it clear that I only had the haziest idea of what your job involved, so trying to pump me about it would have got him nowhere and might have aroused suspicions which hadn't existed before.'

'And, knowing your threshold of suspicion, I applaud his judgement.'

'Me too, because it had been aroused already by something else. Jimmie said that when he told his father during dinner that you were a policeman, he started like a guilty thing upon a dreadful summons, but Mr God gave me a different version.'

'What was that?'

'He said it was Irene Gayford who told him who you were.'

'Did he, indeed?'

'Yes, and the construction I put on that is that it really was Jimmie who told him and that, as a result, he instinctively saw you as someone to be on his guard against. But a few minutes later, when they had moved to the bar, Irene told him she'd recognised you as the Inspector who'd been in charge of the murder case. So that made everything all right again. If you were here in some official capacity, it must have some connection with the earlier case, which neither was, nor ever had been, any concern of his, so he could stop worrying. The next thing is, of course, that I come bobbing along and undo all the good work, and off he goes into another flat spin. Don't you think that would explain it?'

'Not really, no.'

'Why not?'

'Because, if Miss Gayford did tell him that she had recognised me when I came into the dining room, she's most likely a frantic liar.'

'But you recognised her?'

'Only because I've seen her photograph so often and I've been trained to remember details of that kind, as part of my job, but we never came face to face. Someone else further down the line had the job of taking her statement. I knew her name and all about her position in the firm, but that was conveyancing and it very rarely brought her into contact with Pauline. Pauline worked, and always had done, for Young Mr Winthrop. I interviewed him, of course, on several occasions, as well as some of the other members of the staff, particularly those who were friendly with her outside the office, but I never once spoke to Miss Gayford.'

'All the same, she could often have seen you coming and going.'

'No, not often. Most of the interrogation was done in people's homes.'

'Well, perhaps she has one of those photographic memories; once seen, never forgotten.'

'Maybe, or maybe Jimmie told her who I was and she passed it on to Godstow. I'm inclined to take everything that young man says with a pound of salt. Anyway, I don't suppose it's important.'

'Ironic, though, isn't it? You come here to lay that ghost, by one means or another, and all it does it to keep jumping out at you round every corner.'

'And I'm getting tired of it. Tonight was the last straw. And another thing I didn't come here for was cold ham and salad. What do you say we cut our losses and move?'

In the perverse way in which things so often turn out in life, it was now I who felt a reluctance to leave, although I should have found it hard to explain why. I heard myself making feeble excuses about the impracticability of exchanging the devil we knew for a devil as yet unnamed, and pretending that Jimmie would be driven to suicide if we did not turn up at the theatre, but I am sure we both knew it was nonsense. In the end we compromised by agreeing to give it another twenty-four hours and then to decide whether or not to stay for the races.

DAY THREE

(1)

BY NINE o'clock on Wednesday morning another bout of wavering had set in, with the discovery that during the night it had started to rain. The valley was shrouded in a grey woollen blanket, with the sheep buried somewhere inside it, and the rain dripped remorselessly down into the puddles on the drive. Staring out morosely at this dismal scene, my eye was caught by a small green van, parked just below the window and proclaiming itself to be the property of Messrs Denny and Fairbrother, Heating Engineers of Chissingfield.

Turning round, I said to Robin, who had spent the past five minutes staring morosely into the mouthpiece of a dead and silent telephone:

'Well, at least Anthony will be pleased.'

'Why? What have we ever done to him?'

'He wouldn't have been able to run his horse if the ground hadn't softened up a bit. What game are you playing with that telephone?'

'I am trying to ring Reception, to ask Verity to be so kind as to order us some breakfast. She does not answer.'

'I expect they're all busy pouring incense over the man who has come to mend the stove.'

'Including the receptionist?'

'Oh, certainly, if he happens to be good looking.' Being more inhibited than me about appearing in public in *déshabillé*, it took him another ten minutes to make himself presentable enough to go downstairs and start the wheels turning. There was then another yawning interval, followed by a knock on the door, which, to my chagrin, did not herald the arrival of steaming coffee, but Toby, who could find nothing better to do than stare at me morosely.

'There is no reply from Reception,' he informed me.

'Never mind, Robin is in charge. Did you get a newspaper?'

'No.'

'Neither did we, but there's a radio over there. You could see if it works.'

It was tuned to a local station and the announcer was in the process of winding up the news bulletin. He concluded by saying:

'And here is the main story again. During the night a fire broke out at Poltdean Towers, home of millionaire Denzil Godstow. No details have come in, but it is estimated that a number of valuable works of art have been destroyed. We hope to bring you more on this in our next news at ten o'clock.'

The door opened and Robin appeared, morose as ever, carrying a tray laden with tea bags and an electric kettle.

'This is supposed to be a token,' he announced. 'Breakfast proper is promised downstairs in half an hour. Don't get into a white heat of excitement. Something tells me it may be cold ham.'

'Surely it can't take all that long to unblock a pipe?'

'Oh yes, it can. Lupus has seen to that.'

'That wolf in dog's clothing? What's he done?'

'Bitten a lump out of the engineer's hand. Jake has had to drive him to the doctor to get it stitched up and now they're waiting for the firm to send out a replacement.'

'That decides it,' Toby said. 'I shall be leaving before lunch. If you take my advice, you'll do the same.'

'I am tempted to, I have to admit and so, I suspect, is Tessa, but it seems a bit rough to desert the ship now. They've got enough worries, as it is, and I think we ought to do the decent thing and try to stick it out a bit longer.'

'Have they heard about Mr God's fire yet?' I asked.

'Yes, the radio has been giving it out since seven o'clock. That hasn't exactly cheered them up, either.'

'Well, at least it sounds as though the replacement has arrived,' I said, returning to my look-out, as I heard a car approaching, and just in time to see the headlights come creeping through the sodden mist. 'So, providing someone has had the forethought to put Lupus in chains, we may yet get our bacon and eggs. On the other hand,' I added after a pause, in which the car came to a stop and the lights were switched off, 'we may not. This one looks to me more like a police car and my long experience in these matters tells me that it's a plainclothes policeman who is now getting out of it. Let's get a move on, shall we? I can't wait to get downstairs and find out what hell has broken loose now.'

(2)

'Too late!' Robin told me, when I joined him half an hour later in the dining room. 'The visitor has departed.'

'I know, I saw him go while I was doing my face, so there was no point in hurrying. What was it all about, do you know?'

'No, most disappointing. No one has been dragged away in handcuffs, not even Lupus, unfortunately, and all the management and staff appear to be present, if not entirely correct. Presumably, he simply came to verify that Mr God was here while his house was being burnt down, though why that should be necessary I am unable to tell you. This is real coffee, by the way, it hasn't come out of a bag.'

'Does anyone know when the fire started?'

'It must have been during the time we were undergoing that painful session in the bar. It had got a real hold by the time the party arrived home just after two.'

'Hadn't anyone reported it?'

'No, but that's not so surprising. The house stands in its own extensive grounds, as the estate agents are fond of saying, although one wouldn't expect it to be standing in someone else's grounds, and the nearest building is a farm-house, about two miles away.'

'No indoor staff?'

'Not at present. According to Louisa, there's normally a married couple who live in a flat over the garage, but one of their offspring has been lying at death's door in Portugal and they weren't due back until today.'

'Perhaps the police suspect arson and it was the Fellowes they came to see this morning? You know, looking for similarities between their fire and this one. Although it's hard to see what they could have to tell, seeing they were both out of the country when it happened.'

A few minutes later Avril answered some of these questions herself, having first appeared in the doorway, surveying the scene, before walking over to our table.

'Oh, please don't get up!' she begged, putting a hand on Robin's shoulder, presumably to make it plain that she was the kind of woman for whom men did get up, even when heavily engaged in eating fried eggs. 'What a perfectly sickening day, isn't it?'

'Awful! Tessa and I had overlooked the possibility that it might rain on our holiday. We've been wondering how to adapt to it. Will you have some coffee? Toby isn't down yet, so there's plenty in the pot.'

'Thank you, no. I've had my ration for this morning. Yes, it must be dreadfully disheartening for you. There's a National Trust place not far from here, which you might find worth a visit. At least, you'd be under cover.'

'What is there to see there?'

'Oh, just some rather beautifully preserved old barns, which have been turned into a kind of rustic museum. You know the kind of thing, I'm sure? Wooden ploughs and curious shaped lumps of flint, which one couldn't imagine having any useful function. But the barns are superb. They used to be part of the Poltdean estate, which Denzil Godstow now owns, curiously enough, but he very generously handed them over to the Trust. They're some way from the house, so they won't have been affected by the fire, and many people do seem to find them interesting.'

'Is that how you intend to spend the morning?' I asked.

'Oh no, Charles and I have something much more exciting in prospect. At least, we hope it will be. That's why I really wanted a word with your husband, if he can spare a moment?'

'With pleasure!' he assured her. 'Any diversion is most welcome.'

'We've had some amazing news, you see. We still feel there must be some mistake, which is why I was hoping for an expert opinion. We've just had a visit from one of the local bobbies and we can't make it out at all.'

'He brought you some news?'

'Yes, indeed! I'm sure you remember my telling you about our own fire? Nothing on the scale of last night's,, of course, but even so, we lost all our possessions. Some of the outside walls are still intact, but the inside was practically gutted. That's why it took so long to raise the alarm.'

'Yes, it can do a lot of damage, if there's no one at home to smell burning. It was caused by some fault in the wiring, I think you said?'

'That's what they believe. It started in the linen cupboard, of all extraordinary places. If it's true, I'm afraid we have only ourselves to blame. Some of the wiring really was rather old-fashioned and it was silly of us not to have had it seen to, but one tends to put off these things and we were planning to put the house on the market, in any case. It hardly seemed the moment to spend vast sums on inessentials. Neither of our boys, or perhaps I should say our daughters-in-law, had any desire to live there and it was becoming quite impractical to keep it going through the winter. Ironically enough, one of the major expenses was all that electricity burning away, but of course one saw that as a necessary investment.'

'I suppose you had at least moved out all your valuable possessions, though, hadn't you? Either taken them with you, or put them in store?'

'No, Mr Price, foolish as it must sound to you, we hadn't done either of those things. The silver, of course, and some of my jewellery were in the bank; but most of the rest, furniture, pictures, rugs and so forth, had been left just as they were. You may be surprised to hear this, but so few people seem to possess any imagination when it comes to buying a house.

They see stark, empty rooms and they simply cannot visual-ise how they can be made to look when they are furnished.'

Contrary to her expectations, this news came as no surprise to either of us and Robin said:

'I am afraid we have led you away from the point. Didn't you say you had had some news?'

'I did, because it now appears that not all the contents were destroyed, after all.'

'You mean they have turned up alive and well and living somewhere else?'

'Oh, Mr Price, how quick you are! I should hate to be a criminal at your mercy. But I daresay you have known this kind of thing to happen before?'

'Not quite in this way. Were you given any details?'

'We were told that, contrary to what most people believe, a lot of stolen property is sometimes recovered and there have been two cases recently where some quite valuable stuff has been traced back to owners whose houses had been burnt down when they were away, just like ours. So it has become part of the routine to check both kinds of insurance claims, fire as well as theft, when valuable objects are found in suspicious circumstances. Then, if there's any doubt about their origin, they are put on display at the police station and the public can go along and inspect them, if they wish to.'

'So now they think they may have found some of your possessions, which suggests that the house may have been broken into and stripped of its valuables before it caught fire? In other words, that there wasn't necessarily any connection between the two events?'

'So it would appear. Charles is convinced we shall be wasting our time and I expect he is right, but I still think it would be worth while having a look, from curiosity, if nothing else.'

'I don't see how you could resist it,' I told her, 'and, anyway, if you are in luck, I don't see why it should rule out any connection with the fire. Why couldn't one of the burglars have thrown away a lighted cigarette, for instance?'

'Several reasons,' Robin told me, 'one being that professional burglars have more urgent matters to deal with than to stand around chatting and smoking, particularly not in the linen cupboard. There is no possibility, on the other hand, I suppose, that anything could have been pinched from the wreck afterwards? It occurred to me that, if some of your belongings had been stored in the cellar, for instance, they might have escaped damage altogether.'

'No, as I told you, everything was left out, just as though we were still living there. The whole object was to present a home-like effect for the prospective buyers.'

'So that offers another field for speculation, doesn't it? How about these prospective buyers? Who showed them round?'

'It varied, you know. The house could only be viewed by appointment, naturally. My husband's firm had charge of the keys and sometimes one of our sons took the job on. But if people wanted to see the house at the weekend, which they very often did, there was another arrangement.'

'Which was?'

'They had to apply to Mrs Crawley. She was the woman who came in twice a week to dust and air and keep an eye on the place. It wasn't an entirely satisfactory arrangement, because the poor old dear isn't very bright, although no one could be more trustworthy and reliable. She worked for the family for years, until Charles retired. Besides, the vast majority of people who came with orders to view weren't serious buyers at all and one could hardly expect Irene or the boys to sacrifice their weekend to provide them with free Sunday outings.'

'Irene?'

'Gayford. Late of Winthrop and Gayford. The two firms were amalgamated about two years ago. You met her last night.'

'Oh, yes. And so, apart from Mrs Crawley, only those three people had access to the keys?'

'In theory, yes. I suppose almost anyone in the office could have borrowed them, if they'd wanted to, but what difference would that make?'

'None at all, I daresay. All I can tell you is that it is the kind of question that you are likely to be asked, if it should turn out that some of your possessions were removed before the fire started.'

'Oh no, really? But how very unpleasant! You really mean there might be a suggestion that someone we know, one of the employees, could have been involved in a fraud of some kind?'

'I'm only saying that is one line they may decide to pursue.'

'Oh, dear, I don't care for that idea at all. Really, Mr Price, you have spoilt all the fun. I had been so excited by the thought of seeing some of our treasures again, after all this time. Now I can only pray that Charles is right and they will turn out to be someone else's treasures.'

'I'm sorry to be depressing, but you did ask for my opinion.'

'Oh yes, and you mustn't take me seriously, you know. It was just that this has been rather a shock. I had better find Charles and warn him what we may be in for. Oh dear, what a bore it all is, and why does life have to be so complicated?'

'The trouble with people who keep complaining about how bored they are is that they tend to become rather boring,' I remarked.

'Let it be a lesson to you!'

'I'll try to, although I do see that she has more justification than most. It must be intensely boring to have gone to all the trouble and expense of escaping to some tropical paradise, far from the web of crime and intrigue which seems to be so rife in Chissingfield, only to be hauled back into it again through no fault of your own.'

'Unless,' Robin replied, 'they should happen to be two elderly spiders returning to the web to gobble up a few more flies.'

(3)

The reception post was fully manned for once. In fact, keeping up with a trend which I was coming to recognise as the hallmark of this establishment, it had veered towards the opposite extreme and become somewhat overmanned.

Verity was by the switchboard, speaking on the telephone, with Louisa at her side, monitoring the conversation, while Jake, with his back to us, was tapping out a rhythm with one hand and turning the pages of the Visitors' Book with the other.

Louisa turned her head as we reached the foot of the staircase, then, muttering something to the other two, lifted the flap and came towards us, asking if she might have a word.

'Oh, certainly, by all means,' Robin replied without enthusiasm, and I guessed that he too was wondering why 'a word' in this context should inevitably mean an unpleasant one. No one ever asks for a word in order to tell you that you look gorgeous, or have won a Weekend for Two in the Christmas raffle.

'Perhaps if we might pop up to your room for a second? I won't keep you long, but I'm afraid we have a slight panic on our hands,' Louisa explained, treading another well worn path. 'Too bad your cousin had to dash away like that,' she added as we trailed upstairs again.

'Toby? You mean he's left?'

'Yes, but he mentioned something about coming back this evening, Verity tells me. Didn't you know? I suppose the silly girl forgot to pass on the message. Sorry about that, but we've got rather a lot on at the moment.'

We had reached the door of Number Two by this time and she stood aside to allow me to go first. Entering the room, I let out a wild scream, as Lupus leapt off the bed and sprang towards me, all fangs bared.

'Get out, you brute!' she said, giving it a friendly cuff to speed it on its way, whereupon it changed in a flash from bully to coward and slunk out of the room.

'No need to be scared,' she assured me airily, 'he's perfectly harmless, if you know how to treat him.'

'I am not in the least scared. Just faintly taken aback to find him occupying my bed, particularly as I understand he has already bitten a lump out of an electrician this morning.'

'Silly clot! Stuck out his hand to stroke him. You should never do that to alsatians, it makes them nervous.'

'I shall try to remember,' I told her.

'Was there something you wished to say to us?' Robin asked, bringing this polite exchange to a close.

'Yes, that's right. Mind if I sink down and take the weight off my feet for a minute? Well, here goes! The thing is, you see, we've run into a bit of a problem. I expect you heard about the fire last night?'

'Yes, we did. Very bad luck and you must feel particularly sorry about it, in view of the fact that it started while the owner was having dinner here?'

'You can say that again! And the worst of it is that we've now got to do a major reorganisation in double quick time. Panic stations all round.'

Guessing what was coming, I asked: 'Does Mr Godstow now intend to move in here, then?'

'Yes, and we're delighted to have him, of course; and one can quite see that it doesn't suit him to go back to London, with the races coming up next weekend, but it puts us in a bit of a fix. We were pretty booked up for those two nights. Jake and Verity are working on it now; trying to find an excuse to put people off, without giving offence.'

'Not an enviable job,' Robin said, 'and now, I suppose, you're looking for one to use on Tessa and me?'

'Oh gosh, no, such an idea never entered our heads. It's bad enough having to send our reputation up the spout with strangers, not specially recommended people like you two. And that includes your cousin, of course. The only thing is, though, you did say when you booked in that it might be for two nights and I wondered whether you'd come to any decision about that?'

'Yes, we have. Perhaps I should have confirmed it with you, but since we're now into the third day and I haven't asked for our bill, I took it for granted that we could keep the rooms on.'

'Oh yes, of course, couldn't be more delighted, in fact,' Louisa assured us, looking most unhappy about it.

'And, as you were kind enough to ask us to let you know if there was anything we needed,' he continued, sparing her nothing, 'perhaps it would be possible to find a few more coat hangers, which have been promised us several times, but have never arrived.'

'Oh dear, no one told me, I'm so sorry. I'll see to it right away. Anything else?'

'Only some sheets, if it wouldn't be any trouble?'

'Sheets?'

'Yes, the beds look as though they've been made, but in fact there are no sheets on them.'

She had begun to look so terrified of what he might throw at her next that I took pity on her:

'Oh, don't worry, Louisa, I'm sure it was only a misunderstanding. Did my cousin say why he had to go hurtling off like that, do you know?'

'Only that he'd rung his housekeeper to ask if there were any messages and she'd told him about something which had cropped up and he had to deal with right away. He did say he hoped to be back this evening, though, and you were all going to the theatre.'

'So perhaps all he wanted was a square meal?' I suggested. 'I suppose imaginary telephone calls to Mrs Parkes are the modern equivalent of sending oneself a telegram.'

'Don't blame him. I've often been tempted to send myself one.'

'Honestly, Robin, I don't understand you. Now you say you'd welcome an excuse to leave and yet a minute ago, when Louisa handed you one on a silver platter, you turned it down.'

'That was because I don't like being pushed around. They were on their knees to us when we first arrived. Now they've had a better offer, we can shove off and spend the rest of our holiday in a caravan, for all they care. I don't approve of such methods and I'm not having it.'

I accepted this explanation, which sounded irrational enough to be true, although suspecting there might be another incentive at work too. Perhaps, like mine, his reluctance to leave sprang partly from the fact that life at Mattingly Grange was turning out to be so much more eventful than either of us had anticipated.

(4)

After the fortieth ring I was ready to give up, but Robin said I should learn to be patient, so I persevered and finally heard the click and a voice saying:

'Oh, do go away, Tessa, you're driving me mad.'

'And what about me? Off you hop, without a word of warning, the minute my back is turned and then you have the effrontery to say it's me driving you mad.'

'Well, as you know, I'm a moral coward and, if I'd made my departure in a civilised way, you'd have bullied me into changing my mind. Anyway, what have you got to complain about? Robin's still there, isn't he?'

'Just. And you're driving him mad too. For one thing, there's this theatre this evening. We'll have to let the box office know, if we can't use your seat. And that's not all. Louisa is nagging us to death about whether your room is likely to be back on the market.'

'Oh, don't be silly! She must know it will be paid for, whether I use it or not. As there are vast wastes of empty rooms which she hasn't a hope of being paid for, she ought to see it as a bonus.'

'The situation has changed. It is now panic stations all round and her reproachful eyes follow us everywhere. It almost spoilt our lunch, which would have been a pity because it was right back on form. The stove has been repaired and Mr God is here to ensure that the highest standards are kept up.'

'I begin to see! That's the reason for all the hysteria, is it?'

'Yes, and there's any amount of drama going on, one way and another. You'd be a fool to miss it.'

'And an even bigger fool, I daresay, to believe a word of it. Still, it's nice to be wanted and Mrs Parkes didn't look quite so delighted to see me as I'd expected. I'd forgotten that she'd planned to invite her sister to stay while I was away and they thought they were off to spend tomorrow at the Windsor Safari Park. What time does this thing start tonight?'

'Seven thirty.'

'Oh, all right, I might see you then, or in the first interval. And in return for that, Tessa, there's something you can see to right away, if you want to undo some of the havoc you've caused.'

'Anything you say!'

'Explain to Louisa that my reason for leaving was that Mrs Parkes had reminded me that I had an appointment with my doctor this afternoon. It's good news. I'm to come off the diet right away and start building myself up. Calories are what I need now and the more the better.'

In fact, to our relief, he did not turn up until ten minutes into the interval. There was only one and it lasted for an hour, enabling the audience to eat its dinner either in the barn, which had been transformed into a candlelit restaurant, or from picnic baskets in the walled garden.

Relief came from two causes, one being that the production rarely rose to the level of mediocrity, many of the cast being inaudible, even to those who knew the words by heart and in a theatre the size of a doll's house.

Furthermore, as the aggregate was roughly three roles to each player, we were faced with the prospect of listening to them being inaudible later on as different characters. Also, had he arrived on time, he would have seen the slip of paper which fell out of the programme, informing us that the part of Jacques in this performance would be taken by someone with the unpromising name of Peregrine Holt.

'Don't say a word,' I muttered to Robin before the house lights went down. 'With all that costume and wig, he won't know the difference.'

'Won't he find out, though, when we go round afterwards and are greeted by Peregrine instead of Jimmie?'

'No, he hates going round afterwards, so we'll say it's not on because Jimmie has to dress in a broom cupboard, with five others, which is quite likely to be true, and he'll swallow it gratefully.'

It had stopped raining soon after we set out on this expedition, which was fortunate because Robin had now become single-minded about getting his last pennyworth and had requested Louisa to provide us with a picnic dinner, stipulating only that it should not include cold ham, or anything distantly related to it. This embargo had received due attention and once again the management of Mattingly Grange had looked around for the opposite extreme and found it.

One observer, a handsome, middle-aged, friendly looking woman, who strolled across to talk to us while we were digging into the *saumon en croute*, was much impressed:

'You two do yourselves well,' she remarked. 'That's what I call a spread.'

'We've got Toby's share here too, you see,' I explained, 'why don't you join us? There's more than enough, if he does come, and we can't take it with us. I wouldn't dare, in case Robin demanded a rebate. There's a macintosh under this rug, so you won't get pneumonia, or ruin your dress. You remember Robin, don't you?' I added, as she hastened to avail herself of the invitation.

Although it was some years now since we had met, I did not consider it necessary to remind him that she was Roberta Grayle, known to a million friends as Bobbie. Nor was it, and he declared himself to be delighted to see her.

'And what brings you here on such a night?' I enquired. 'Not snooping on Peregrine, by any chance? Judging by his performance as Le Beau in Act One, Jimmie hasn't a thing to worry about.'

'I know that, darling and so does he. It's you two he's worried about. I am here to apologise for this unfortunate absence. I, on the other hand, am inclined to be worried about him. It is becoming rather like *La Ronde* in a rustic setting.'

'What's the matter? Is he ill?'

'Not exactly, although in a certain amount of pain, I gather. Tell me something, just between ourselves; did he have rather a lot to drink last night?'

'I wouldn't have said so, Bobbie. He was sober enough when we said goodnight to him and he was on the point of leaving then.'

'What time was that?'

'About eleven, wouldn't you say, Robin?'

'Not later, certainly. Are you worried because he's suffering from what appear to be symptoms of a hangover?'

'No, he's hurt his wrist. Or so he says.'

'And how does he say he did it?'

'That when he was on his way home the car went into a skid and, in wrenching the steering wheel round, to try and pull out of it, he somehow managed to sprain his wrist. His left one, fortunately.'

'A likely tale, in your opinion?'

'I don't see why, though,' Robin objected. 'There's no denying that it must have started to bucket with rain at some point during the night and that can make the roads very tricky, especially after a long dry spell like we've just had.'

'Yes, I know.'

'So why not believe him?'

'Oh, just me being silly old mother hen, I suppose, but one begins to sense when people one knows well are lying, don't you find?'

'I wouldn't know,' I told her, with a glance at Robin, who said:

'And so you suspect that it may have been more serious than he pretends and he made up this story so as not to worry you? If so, he can hardly claim to have succeeded. Is the car all right?'

'Not a scratch, and that's another funny thing. I mean, do you honestly believe that a strong man could sprain his wrist simply by wrenching the wheel round? Wouldn't it take some kind of jolt, as well?'

'Such as a sharp collision with an immovable object, for instance?'

'Right. And furthermore, if one had sprained one's wrist, would one just wrap it up in about twelve yards of bandage and stick it in a home made sling? Wouldn't one be more likely to hurry round to the doctor to make sure no bones were broken?'

'One might well,' I agreed, 'but I still don't see what difference it would make if one were drunk or sober when it happened.'

'None at all to most people, but you see I'm stuck with the hideous phobia about alcohol and no one knows it better than Jimmie. I signed my own private pledge years ago. It's not much use trying to persuade someone else to lay off, if you're fortifying yourself with a swig or two while preaching about it. That's why it occurred to me that Jimmie might have been plastered last night and then got mixed up in some brawl. It would be just like his mean-spirited old crook of a father to egg him on to something like that. Still, you tell me it wasn't so, and I expect I'm making far too much of it. Just put it down to paranoia.'

'Have you met his father?'

'Only once and it was a disaster. I am obviously not his type.'

'Is he really a crook?'

'No, I shouldn't think so, I'm only repeating what Jimmie has told me and no one could claim that he has an open mind on that subject. The big surprise is that he should have consented to go to the party at all. I suppose the poor old darling saw it as an olive branch and was too good natured to throw it back where it came from.'

'Where is Jimmie now?' Robin asked.

'At home with Max. And by home I mean just down the road. It was too far for him to drive to London every night, so the three of us have rented a cottage here for the season. You must come over and have lunch one day while you're here. I should warn you, though, that it won't be up to this standard,' she added, helping herself to another dollop of iced pudding.

Luckily, despite her hearty appetite, there was still a respectable amount left when Toby arrived by taxi a few minutes later. He was full of complaints, as usual, and we might have spent what remained of the interval in listening to them, had not Robin, in one of his brilliant flashes of genius, pointed out that Jimmie's sprained wrist absolved us from the necessity of going back into the theatre at all.

Elation was short lived, however, because we had reckoned without Bobbie. Either because her heart was large enough to embrace the entire population of southern England, or because anything which affected Jimmie's interests, however remotely, had to be protected, she refused to allow such backsliding. Reminding us that the gaping hole left by three empty seats in the fifth row could only demoralise the cast still further, she brought the rebellion to an end.

The first part of the journey home passed merrily enough in tearing the production to pieces and then reassembling it, in order to repeat the process from another point of view. When that topic was exhausted, we moved on to the mysterious behaviour of Jimmie and his sprained wrist. Toby, to whom all this came as news, was not disposed to treat it seriously.

'Quite simple,' he announced, 'he used the first excuse that came into his retarded little head not to go on tonight and, for once, I do not blame him.'

'You may be right,' I admitted, 'it does sound like that, but all the same it's out of character. Retarded or not, he's still a pro and he'd rather be seen in fifth-rate surroundings than not be seen at all.'

'On the other hand,' Robin said, 'whatever he may or may not have done to his wrist, I doubt very much if he has sprained it.'

'Why?'

'Because Bobbie told us it was his left one.'

'And?'

'You might conceivably get away with steering right handed only, if you were cautious, but with a right hand drive it's the left one which has to do all the work.'

'How about if it was an automatic?'

'This one isn't. My copper's eye is trained to pick out such trivia and last night Jimmie was driving an ancient Triumph convertible. Automatic gears had scarcely been heard of when that model was built.'

'There now!' I said. 'And just fancy! I think I'll ring him up in the morning and tease him a bit. The more he goes on about how his wrist is quite all right now, thank you, the more I'll keep insisting that he ought to get it X-rayed.'

'You'd better watch it!' Robin said, turning into our tree-lined drive. 'One of these days your sadistic sense of humour will get you into trouble.'

I did not take this warning seriously and I daresay I was not intended to, but all the same the threat was never carried out. The morning was to provide more interesting events to occupy the mind, and the subject of Jimmie and his sprained wrist was temporarily relegated to the miscellaneous memory file.

DAY FOUR. MORNING AND AFTERNOON

(1)

BY THURSDAY morning everything, on the surface at any rate, was back to normal at Mattingly Grange. The sun shone, the breakfast trolley had been wheeled in on time and the sheep were once more visible from the windows of Numbers Two and Three.

'So what shall we do this morning?' Robin asked.

'It is not an easy decision. The choice seems to lie between tramping round some ancient barns, scouring Chissingfield for knitting wool, or checking on progress in the summer house. Perhaps it would be more amusing to stay here and track down Mrs Fellowes. I am keen to hear about yesterday's expedition.'

'It was really quite sinister and depressing,' she informed us when we had tracked her down to the terrace, where she sat plying her needle and looking more ambassadorial than ever in a lavender coloured dress and double row of pearls. She also reminded me of the Lady of Shalott, for she had her back to the garden and all she could see of it was the blurred and broken reflection in the plate glass windows.

'One hardly knows whether to laugh or cry,' she added, not looking ready to do either.

'You mean nothing came of it?' Robin asked.

'Oh, something came of it, yes indeed, but quite the last thing one would have wished. Charles is taking his mind off things with a round of golf,' she explained, floating off on another tack. 'So sensible of him, but really I begin to wonder how long we shall be able to go on like this. We seem to keep moving round in circles and getting nowhere. It is all so frustrating and boring.'

Her special brand of evasiveness, taking the form of speaking at length without saying anything, was beginning to wear me down, but Robin was made of sterner stuff:

'So none of your property has turned up, after all? Perhaps that is a relief, in one sense?'

'No, my dear, it wasn't as simple as that. If only it had been!'

He did not comment and, evidently deciding that she was now in danger of losing her audience, she went on: 'We did find some of our belongings, you see, but nothing of any value, apart from the sentimental one. So now we are in the horrid position of having to accept that the fire was not the straightforward affair we had supposed it to be, without the compensation of recovering some of our treasures.'

'What kind of things were they?' I asked.

'High class junk is really the best way to describe them. The only one I was happy to see again was the patchwork quilt my grandmother made for her trousseau. Apart from that, there was a Victorian china washstand set and one or two engravings of the same period. Then there was rather a hideous art nouveau lamp, a little silver cigar cutter and an ivory chess set, which was probably the only thing of any real value. Oh, and a collection of medals, believe it or not!'

'Medals?'

'Yes, we used to keep them inside a glass topped table. They'd all been acquired by members of Charles's family, from the Boer War down to the last one. Curious thing to steal, don't you think? But we were told there is quite a demand for them among collectors.'

'Which also applies to the other things you've mentioned,' Robin told her. 'Junk to you, maybe, but there's a thriving market for it now. So much so that it's become worthwhile to mass produce copies.'

'And where was it found?' I asked, 'or didn't they tell you?'

'It was part of a consignment which was on its way to France. All I can say is that I wish it had got there, instead of falling off a lorry into the hands of the police. Now we're faced with having to find a home for the poor things, which can only lead to more trouble and expense and another round of wrangles with the insurance company. Such a bore!'

'Not to mention,' Robin reminded her, 'the still more tricky questions of how these odds and ends survived the fire.'

'You're so right, Mr Price, but I must tell you of a little theory Charles has about that. He'd be too shy to mention it himself, but I'd be so interested to hear your views, if I haven't bored you enough already with our troubles?'

'Not in the least bored,' I assured her. 'Other people's troubles tend to be so much more amusing than one's own, don't you think?'

'Well, if your husband agrees that Charles could be right about this, it will at least mean the end of one of our troubles, which would be some comfort. What he believes, you see, is that although it was not reported at the time, these bits and pieces did somehow escape the fire and were removed after it was put out. In other words, a little light looting.'

'By members of the Fire Brigade, you mean?'

'I suppose it would have to be them, wouldn't it? Could such a thing be possible?'

'I wouldn't have thought so. Did your husband suggest it to the police?'

'No, I advised him not to. I thought it best to consult you first and find out what their reaction was likely to be.'

'I suppose a lot would depend on what evidence you have to back it up.'

'Oh, none whatever. What evidence could we have when we were out of the country?'

'That wouldn't necessarily make any difference. For instance, one very obvious question is, had these things been lumped together in one room in a part of the house which was relatively undamaged, or were they spread around?'

'I don't know that I can tell you offhand. Perhaps one of the boys would remember. I could ask them.'

'I would, if I were you because it could be vital. One could conceivably imagine someone snatching up a few trifles close to hand, after the job was finished. Improbable, I should have said, but conceivable. Whereas, to have made a tour of the premises, scavenging anything which remained intact, would have been far more complicated. At the very least, it would have required the rest of the team to turn a blind eye. The more logical conclusion has to be that they were all involved, and that does seem a bit far-fetched. Still, if you think this is what may have happened, I would certainly advise you to lodge a complaint. I can assure you that it will be very thoroughly investigated and no effort spared to find the culprit.'

He was beginning to sound more like an Inspector interrogating a hostile witness than someone engaged in conversation with a fellow guest and he evidently had a similar effect on Mrs Fellowes, for she said:

'Oh dear, that doesn't sound very pleasant. Rather like taking a sledge hammer to crush a walnut. I shall definitely advise Charles to think no more about it. Obviously, the most sensible thing is to accept our few crumbs and ask no questions. Oh, my goodness, and now I seem to be running out of pink embroidery silk. I shall have to make the effort to go upstairs and rout around for some more.'

'Well, you certainly told her off that time,' I said. 'You sounded a bit like a sledge hammer yourself.'

'I meant to. Tiresome woman! Who does she think I am?'

'I don't know, Robin. Who is she meant to think you are?'

'Not the half wit she apparently took me for. Did you ever hear such a farrago? She might at least have paid me the compliment of inventing a slightly more plausible tale than that.'

'Was it the veiled accusations against the brave men of the Fire Brigade which annoyed you so much?'

'And not so veiled either, were they? You'll have noticed that when I asked her outright if her husband believed they were responsible, she made no attempt to deny it?'

'Well, naturally you're prejudiced in their favour and quite right too, but is it to be completely ruled out? Supposing all that junk had been collected in one room, which hadn't been so badly damaged as the rest, and one of them had noticed this at the time. Isn't it possible that he could have come back later and packed them into his own car?'

'Rather a risky errand for such a trivial reward, wouldn't you say? And you seem to have forgotten an earlier conversation we had with her, before they knew anything had been salvaged. At that time she told us repeatedly that everything had been left just as though they were still living there.'

'No, I hadn't forgotten.'

'So it conjures up a peculiar sort of life style, doesn't it? Here we have a room necessarily on the ground floor, since the house was gutted, and these are some of the things it contained: a collection of medals, an ivory chess set and a washstand basin and jug. What kind of a room was that?'

'Well, why not a study or workroom, filled with cast-offs which had been weeded out from other parts of the house, as fashions changed? I rather picture the boys doing their homework there in the evenings.'

'Oh, so do I. I have the complete list of these *objets trouvés* in my mind and I can picture it vividly. There they are, these two rumbustious lads, working away by the light from an art nouveau lamp. When they have finished, they put away their books and wash their inky hands in a china bowl, with water from the matching jug, before taking a brief rest on the patchwork quilt. After that, of course, they feel refreshed enough to light up their cigars, pin on their medals and take each other on at a game of chess. Whyever not?'

'I haven't got your filing cabinet mind, of course, and I must admit that it does sound rather bizarre. On the other hand, Mrs Fellowes seemed uncertain where all these things had been, so perhaps there is some other explanation.'

'Without doubt, there is some other explanation, which is that she had fallen into a trap of her own making. She had realised by then that they could not possibly have been removed unless they had all been together in one room, so she tried to get out of it by pretending that it might have been so. Well, I hope I have brought the curtain down on that little farce. The dress rehearsal having fallen flat on its face, the first night will be postponed, pending further attention to the script.'

'You think that's what it was, then? Just rehearsing on you, to get an audience reaction?'

'Precisely! And I'm getting tired of being the pawn in her ivory chess set.'

'And, after all, why does she bother? Why not just say that they have no idea how these things happen to have been rescued and shut up about it?'

'Because she evidently believes that such a negative reaction would not be enough. For some reason, which she's not telling, it's important to her to root out any suspicion that the house was burnt down after it had been burgled.'

'Yes, but why? That's what I'd like to know.'

'So would I,' Robin said. 'I wouldn't half like to know too.'

(2)

In contrast to its former depressing emptiness, with the arrival of the Godstow contingent Mattingly Grange had become depressingly overpopulated. Only three of them were staying there, these being the host, his daughter and his daughter's friend, the others having been farmed out to a guest house, but their sublime disregard for other people's existence made them as obtrusive as three times that number. They also had the knack of taking over whatever part of the premises they happened to be in, and when Robin and I returned from our obligatory walk round the garden, after our talk with Mrs Fellowes, we were disgusted to find the invaders in full possession of the terrace.

Half the floor space was occupied by Diana and Stephanie, both wearing bikinis and lying face down on inflatable mattresses, apparently with the optimistic intention of acquiring a Moroccan tan from the pale spring sunshine. Still more offensive was the sight of two of the guest house overflow playing backgammon at the very table which, after three days, we had come to regard as our exclusive property.

After a consultation with Toby, we decided to protect ourselves from further outrages of this kind and to spend the day exploring the countryside, the only debatable point being which part of it.

My proposal of seeing what the shops of Taunton had to offer having been outvoted, I next suggested that we should take Roberta up on her invitation to lunch. This found more favour, but also raised a further problem. Robin had now become obsessed by the determination not to allow the management to do him out of so much as a sausage roll and he maintained that, if we were not to eat lunch at the hotel, then the hotel must fulfil the terms of its contract by providing us with lunch to eat elsewhere.

'We could invite Max and Bobbie to a picnic in their own garden,' he suggested. 'Judging by last night's effort, there is sure to be enough to go round and it would be a more gracious way of descending on them at an hour's notice. Let us go and arrange matters with Verity. This happens to be one of the rare mornings when she is on duty. At least, Mr God's presence is keeping the staff on its toes.'

He was right too, and when the smiling, welcoming Verity had made her eager enquiry as to whether there was anything we needed and had been told what it was, she actually remembered that there had been a telephone message for Robin, while we were out on our walk, although unable for the moment to recollect what she had done with it.

'In my pigeon hole, beside the key?' he suggested.

'No, I was going to put it there, naturally, but everything's got a bit out of gear this morning. Let's see now! Perhaps if I try a little total recall, it'll come to me. I do remember that I was talking to Miss Gayford when the phone rang.'

'Miss Gayford?' I repeated. 'Don't tell me she's moved in here too?'

'Oh no, God forbid, but she's mislaid a pair of specs and she thought they might have dropped out of her bag when she was dining here. Which reminds me, I must remember to ask Kenneth about it some time. They haven't turned up in the dining room, but I suppose she might have left them in the bar.'

'In the meantime. . . .' Robin said.

'Yes, that's right, your message. Oh, just look, staring us in the face!' she said, opening the Visitors' Book and removing a slip of paper, which looked as though it had been put there to mark the place. 'Let's see now! It came through at nine forty-five, or as near as, and was to ask you to ring this number as soon as you came in.'

'No name?' Robin asked, when he had read it for himself.

'Sorry, no, he didn't give his name.'

'But it was a man?'

'Oh yes, and another thing I can tell you is that it's the Chissingfield code number.'

'How odd! I didn't think I knew anyone in Chissingfield . . . unless, of course . . . Well, the only thing is to find out, isn't it? Would it be all right to use this telephone while you fly about organising our picnic? If anyone comes, we'll tell them you'll be back in five minutes.'

Verity did not look too pleased to be given her flying orders in this way, but the motto of the house prevailed and she sauntered away towards the kitchen.

'And, if they should need their keys, or any little service of that kind,' Toby remarked, 'Tessa will be here to deal with it.'

Robin, having dialled the number, waited for half a minute, then replaced the receiver, lifted it again and dialled the same number, with the same negative result.

'Did you think it might be the local police station?' I enquired.

'Quite right, it did seem the only answer. Can't be, though. At least, I hope not, since there seems to be no one there.'

'Unless, of course, Verity wrote it down wrongly?'

'And why wouldn't she? You'd better ring Roberta and warn her what's in store, while I look them up in the book.'

Two minutes later I reported: 'They're at home and looking forward to seeing us. How about yours?'

'No go. The number is so entirely different that not even Verity could have confused them. Never mind, I'll try again this evening.'

The flyer returned with the news that our picnic baskets would be ready in half an hour and the request to Robin to hand over his car keys. Jake would then personally ensure that everything was packed in the boot right side up.

'What service!' he said, putting them down on the counter.

'Oh well, we aim to please, as they say. Any luck with your call?'

'Unfortunately not. I suppose. . . .'

'Yes?'

'There couldn't be any mistake, could there? I realise you've had a lot of extra work pushed on to you this morning and just wondered if you were absolutely sure the message was for me and not one of the other guests?'

'No, no, I'm quite sure. I distinctly remember that the first thing he asked was whether there was a Mr Robin Price staying here, so I said yes and that you'd gone for a walk and then he asked me to write down the number and read it back to him, as it was rather urgent. So there's no way I could have got it wrong, is there?'

'You sounded quite bothered about it?' I suggested, when we had moved upstairs to study the map and work out a scenic route.

'No, just irritated. Unlike you, I don't care for mysteries.'

'Then I have good news for you,' Toby announced. 'The mystery can be cleared up all too soon for Tessa's liking. Obviously, your caller was Anthony.'

'Anthony Blewiston?'

'That's the one. Didn't you tell me, Tessa, that he had a horse entered for one of the races? What more natural than that he should now get in touch, to announce his presence and find out if you are still here?'

'Several things more natural. One is that he would have asked for her and not me. Another is that he would have given his name; and, if you want me to wrap it up and throw it away, by no stretch of the imagination could he have considered it a matter of urgency that I should ring him back.'

'Well, I can see that you are determined to go on being mystified and irritated, so you must dree your own weir.'

'No, I shall stop being a bore and accept the way you have dreed it for me. It has always been evident that Anthony inhabited an earlier and more chivalrous world than ours and I quite see that he would consider it the height of caddishness to bandy a lady's name on the telephone. I shall think no more about it.'

Such resolutions are easier made than kept, however. This one showed signs of wavering during the first part of our drive, steadied itself as we jostled our way down the Chissingfield street market, where the fish and produce stalls were set out cheek by jowl with racks of tatty garments and tables piled high with plastic toys, and fell flat on its face when we arrived at the Grayles' cottage. This was because the first of the three people to leap up from their garden chairs to greet us was my old friend, Anthony Blewiston.

(3)

'Where's your young man?' I asked Bobbie, who had escorted me upstairs for what Louisa would have called a scrub up.

'Got a matinée, poor old lamb.'

'So he's recovered from his injuries?'

'Not entirely. He's still got the bandage on, but it won't show under all those cuffs and gauntlets. The sling has been discarded. He's had to give up that silly pretence.'

'Was it a pretence?'

'I'm afraid so. He came down to breakfast wearing, it and Max had to slice up his toast for him and make some brave soldiers to dip in his boiled egg, but unfortunately I was tactless enough to go into the bathroom while he was shaving. He seemed to be managing quite well without it.'

'So what's the game?'

'I really couldn't tell you, Tessa. Maybe just plain old-fashioned lead swinging. Who can say?'

'Because he hates this job he's stuck with at the Old Mill? No one could blame him, but it's not like Jimmie to be unprofessional and let other people down. And it could hardly be to draw attention to himself because, God knows, he gets enough of that from you and Max without even trying.'

'Yes, I know and, in a funny way, he's just as dependent on Max as he is on me. That's probably what most infuriates his real father. Hence my base suspicion that he had set out to get Jimmie drunk at his party. It would be a way of getting back at both of us. However, your saying that he left soon after eleven has given me a different idea.'

'What's that?'

'Well, you see, he wasn't back here until after two. He came in very quietly and he doesn't know I heard him, but when you get to my age the slightest sound can wake you after an hour or two's sleep and I've had more than my share in the past of lying in bed, waiting for the reveller to return in the small hours.'

'But if he's under the illusion that you don't know what time he came in, why this elaborate pretence of having damaged his wrist? What would be the point of that?'

'Oh, I'm certain he did hurt himself in some way and that he genuinely was in pain the next morning. What I don't believe is that it happened in the way he described. There's something going on that he doesn't want me to know about. Some young lady at the bottom of it, I shouldn't wonder.'

'Why on earth should you say that?'

'Well, it's happened before, you know, more than once. It seems to coincide with the Galahad mood, funnily enough. Perhaps it makes a nice occasional change from being the beamish boy at home.'

'What does the Galahad mood do for him?'

'Oh, you know, Tessa! Taking up with some girl who's had a rotten deal, or unhappy childhood, or something. Two or three years ago, I remember there was someone. It didn't last, they never do, but this one became pregnant, or said she had, and got it into her head they were going to be married, which scared him right off. He's much too immature for the husband and father role. Still, he was bound to grow up one day and I shouldn't complain. I've had a good innings, as you cricket fans say, and I must learn how to leave the field gracefully, if the time for that is now coming.'

I did not argue with her because, much as I regretted it, I had to admit that she was probably right, so I moved on to the subject of Anthony and she said:

'We didn't know he was coming until he rang up last night. It was a lovely surprise. I hadn't seen him since he gave up the unequal struggle to be an actor, but Max ran into him in London the other day, when he was lunching with his publisher, and he must have given him our telephone number. He doesn't remember doing so, but you know how flustered he always gets on these occasions? Goes burbling on, out of sheer nerves and half the time he has no idea what he's saying. Anyway, it's fun to see Anthony again and he seems much happier now that he's so rich.'

'Where was he ringing from? Chissingfield?'

'No, Sussex. He started out at six this morning and arrived here a few minutes before you did.'

'Could it really take him so long?'

'Every bit. He came in his Land Rover, with the head lad and the horse box behind, so they couldn't do more than forty miles an hour.'

'Is he staying with you?'

'No, I think he may have been fishing for an invitation, but we simply haven't room. Max had offered to drive him over to Chissingfield this afternoon, but perhaps you could take him instead? Poor Anthony, he's had a run of bad luck.'

'Why, what's happened to him?'

'He'd been invited to stay with some of his grand friends, but a day or two ago his hostess fell off her horse and broke her pelvis, so that's out. Then he tried the place where you're staying, but he'd no sooner got that all fixed when they rang him back to say there'd been some muddle over the bookings and they hadn't got a room for him, after all. Now he's hoping to get in at some little pub he knows. Not that it bothers Anthony where he stays. He wouldn't miss this meeting, if it meant spending the night in the horse box.'

'Where do you want to be dropped?' Robin asked him.

'Just the other side of Chissingfield, if you'd be so kind, old boy. Little dump called the Weston Arms. Bit out of the way, I'm afraid, but we don't need to go through the town. I can show you the back doubles.'

'I've heard of the Weston Arms,' I said, 'but blowed if I can remember where or when.'

'You must be one of the few. It hasn't much of a reputation nowadays. Neither quaint nor comfortable, if you follow me? Still, as long as they can find a bed for me, that's all that matters.'

'All the same, I wish I could remember who was telling me about it. It's going to annoy me.'

'Think about something else and it'll come to you in a blinding flash. On second thoughts, Robin, old scout, it might be a good idea to go through the town, after all, if it's not asking too much of you?'

'No, it isn't, but why?'

'Just had a blinding flash myself and realised that when I get to this hostelry, which shall be nameless out of consideration to Tessa, I shall be minus transport. Damn nuisance, really, but things haven't worked out according to plan and I was unprepared for this contingency.'

'Doesn't bother me, Anthony, but how does it help to go through Chissingfield?'

'I've got an old friend there, name of Mahomed, who runs a garage. He might be able to fix me up with some broken-down old hire car.'

Curiously enough, this was the very topic to distract my tortured mind from the Weston Arms. I had already been suffering pangs of guilt over the fact that Robin and I were luxuriating in two enormous rooms, while Anthony was obliged to doss down in some back street hovel, but had been unable to see a way out of it. To have suggested that he take over part of our premises would have brought fierce opposition from Robin, who would inevitably have seen it as a means whereby the hotel could wring an extra and unfair profit and it might not have done Anthony any good either. There was a fair chance that it would end with one or more of the Godstow party moving in and sharing our bathroom.

I now saw a better way to make amends and I said: 'It seems silly to hire a car when we have two between the three of us. Why not borrow one of ours?'

It is always a pleasure, of course, to lend other people's property in a deserving cause and, although neither Robin nor Toby appeared to be ecstatic about my offer, I was able to shame them into endorsing it. So we made straight for the hotel, removed the picnic baskets, and Anthony drove off to his elusively named destination. The minute he had gone Robin said: 'Damnation!'

'What's the matter now?'

'I've left my . . . something in the car.'

'Something you need?'

'Something I wouldn't want to fall into the wrong hands. Or into any hands, for that matter.'

'Where did you leave it? In the boot?'

'Yes. Having noticed the somewhat easy-going attitude to keys in this establishment, I decided that would be the safest place for it. Oh well, never mind! Anthony's bound to remember to lock the car, when he's found somewhere to park it.'

'He's left his number, so you could ring him up and remind him to.'

'I will, but he won't be there yet and, anyway, I have something more important to do first.'

DAY FOUR. EVENING

(1)

IMPORTANT or not, it availed him nothing, for there was still no reply from the Chissingfield number.

Robin toyed with the idea of putting Verity on the carpet and grilling her about whether she had written it down correctly, but soon realised that this would be another waste of time. Further evidence of how far he had been subverted by the unwinding process came from the fact that it was not until later that he realised that far more reliable sources of information were open to him and, even then, he was reluctant to use them.

'It could lead to all kinds of farcical complications,' he explained. 'Supposing, for instance, that Verity had got it wrong and the number belongs to someone who has never heard of me? I should look a prize ass calling all that machinery into play to no purpose whatever and it could cause hideous embarrassment to some innocent householder. The very thing to sour relations between the public and police.'

'Oh, but wouldn't they be discreet about it? Is there any reason why the innocent householder should ever know?'

'Maybe not, but I still feel inclined to drop it. The annoying thing is, there was something vaguely familiar about that number, but if it was really urgent and really me he wanted, there's nothing to stop him trying again, is there? The best thing is to put it out of my mind. Besides, Anthony may have arrived at his pub now, so at least I can get that business sorted out. He'll curse me, I expect, but I think the safest bet would be for him to take it out of the car and keep it by him. Nothing like race meetings for bringing out the car thieves and then I really should have egg on my face.'

Half an hour later a call came through on my bedroom extension and Anthony said:

'Hallo! Is your old man there?'

'Downstairs in the bar. I could get you transferred, if you have an hour or two to spare, but perhaps you'd rather I took a message?'

'Just put it as tactfully as only you know how, that he's losing his marbles.'

'Okay. Is that all?'

'If more is required, you can say that at six twenty-five, acting on instructions, I proceeded to the Municipal Car Park, where I had left the vehicle in question, in an attempt to retrieve the article he had described from the rear luggage compartment of said vehicle.'

'And then what?' I said, cutting into this somewhat laboured comedy act, which was about on a par with his usual level of performance in days gone by.

'It wasn't there. Neither in the aforementioned luggage compartment, nor anywhere else in said bloody vehicle.'

'You're quite sure?'

'Quite. I examined every inch of it on my hands and knees.'

'I'll tell him. Thanks for letting us know.'

'No trouble. Not much, anyway. See you tomorrow!'

'Yes, but before you hang up, Anthony . . .'

'What now?'

'Two things, actually. The first is what did said article look like?'

'According to the description, much like any other brief case. Flat, black and boring. I could hardly have missed it.'

'No, you couldn't.'

'What's the other one?'

'More of a request this time. If it's all the same to you, it might be as well not to mention, even to your closest friend, that Robin has lost a flat, black and boring brief case.'

(2)

Robin and Toby were the only customers when I joined them in the bar and they were holding a discussion with Kenneth, who had no doubt instigated it for professional purposes, on current American speech. Toby considered himself to be an authority on this subject, Mr and Mrs Parkes having recently been on a package holiday to Florida, an event which had revolutionised the language and customs of his household at Roakes Common. He was explaining the difference between English muffins and the other sort when I arrived, but luckily Mr and Mrs Fellowes were hot on my heels and Kenneth was obliged to descend from these linguistic heights to the mundane world of gin and tonic and dry sherry.

'Bad news!' I told Robin and gave him a paraphrase of Anthony's report. He dismissed it by saying:

'Silly fool! Of course it's there. I saw it myself only . . .'

'When?'

'I'm trying to remember,' he admitted with diminishing confidence. 'Oh yes, when I put the picnic baskets in. I had to move it to make room for one of them. So it must still be there.'

'What must?' Toby asked. 'One thing I do wish you'd remember is to include me in your conversation. Anyone would think I was here for my own pleasure, instead of the selfless cause of saving your marriage.'

'Some papers I left in the car,' Robin explained, 'and where, in a manner of speaking, they had no business to be. In case you're wondering why they were there, I can best describe them as the albatross that's been round my neck ever since we decided to come here. As you know, I was hooked on the idea that by recollecting the past in the tranquillity of a holiday mood, I should hit on something which had passed me by in the heat of battle. With that in mind, I had brought along some files, so that I could check back on various points as they might be resurrected. Those are the files which are now missing.'

'But you're not bothered? You consider it more likely that Anthony is mistaken?'

'If you turn off the lights, you may hear me whistling.'

'All the same, it's possible,' I said. 'He's not terribly bright, except where horses are concerned.'

'Now, that's where I consider you and Robin are mistaken. I think you should try to re-arrange your ideas about him.'

'I'll try anything once, Toby. Where do we begin?'

'As I understand it, as soon as Anthony learnt that Robin had left a brief case in the car, he leapt off to retrieve it, then scuttled back to his pub for a good read.'

'Even so, why would he then say it wasn't there?'

'Because one glance at the papers it contained made it necessary for him to destroy them.'

I was too flabbergasted by this aspersion to utter a word and Robin filled the gap for me.

'Can you be implying that he was involved in some way with the events they relate to?'

'Up to his neck. I would go so far as to say that he has done very well out of it and the last thing he would care for is to have the case re-opened.'

'I never heard anything so preposterous in my life,' I said, stung into speech again. 'In what way has he done very well out of it, I should like to know?'

'The best of all ways. He is now a rich man and has achieved everything in life which had always seemed beyond his reach.'

'Don't talk piffle! You know very well where his money came from.'

'I know where he says it came from, but I would remind you that it arrived in two instalments, round about the time when your Pauline was murdered.'

'She's not my Pauline, she's Robin's, and you're out of your mind. Just because she was killed during the same year as two elderly spinsters died in their beds is no justification for calling him a liar.'

'It would be easy enough to check whether the elderly spinsters ever existed and, if so, who inherited their money,' Robin said, 'but I agree with Tessa that it would take rather more evidence than a missing brief case to set up enquiries of that kind.'

'Very well, tell me this, Tessa! When you met Anthony in London and told him that you and Robin were planning to come here, what was his reaction? Think carefully, now!'

Having done so, I replied: 'As I told you, he assumed that the holiday was a blind and that the murder investigation was on again.'

'And why was that, you should ask yourself? He may have been here when the murder was committed, almost certainly was, but it is equally certain that he was far away when the news broke and all the locals were talking about it. So why, two years later, should he have made such an assumption, unless it had a particular significance for him?'

'Easy! Knowing all about Robin's job, it was simply an association of ideas.'

'I don't agree, but I'll let it pass because I have another trip down memory lane lined up for you. Before you parted from him in London, did he not tell you that he was planning to enter one of his horses for this meeting? Rather a long way to come, wasn't it, for such a minor event? Isn't it more likely that it was just an excuse to be on the spot and find out as much as he could about what Robin was up to?'

'No, and that's where you really show your ignorance. For horses of that calibre, it's not the location or prize money which matters. It's whether the distance is right and what the competition is likely to be. If those conditions measure up to requirements, people think nothing of taking their horses three or four hundred miles and back again the next day.'

'You had better listen to her, Toby. There is a remote chance that she knows what she is talking about.'

'If it comes to that, so do I, and here is something she may find it more difficult to argue her way out of. Having, for whatever reason, decided to come, the next step is to ensure that he will be staying in the same hotel as you and Robin. This is tricky, though, because you have both heard tales of all the many like-minded cronies in the neighbour-hood who would be only too happy to put him up. So there is the danger that you will be asking yourselves why he should have chosen to dissipate Auntie's money on the exorbi-tant charges of Mattingly Grange, which is several miles from the race course, in the knowledge that he will have no transport to convey him there. He finds the way out of this difficulty by inventing some friends who had invited him to stay, but been obliged to put him off at the last minute. However, as we know, the plan then started to go wrong. Mattingly Grange, which normally can be relied upon for acres of empty rooms, had been invaded by a personage whose goodwill was infinitely more precious than his and they call him back to say that he is not to come, after all.'

'I must admit,' Robin said, voicing a thought which, regrettably, had also occurred to me, 'there was something faintly fishy about that story of the woman falling off her horse and breaking her pelvis. I put it down to the fact that he is such a lousy actor that he can't even make the truth sound convincing.'

'Very likely, my dear, but in this case he was doubly handicapped by the fact that it wasn't the truth. And every-thing I have told you so far makes a neat and logical prelude to the final move in the game.'

'What was that?'

'The telephone call. Naturally, I had no idea then what lay behind it, but obviously it was Anthony, trying to get you to intercede for him and persuade the hotel to find him a room. Naturally, he preferred to remain anonymous while negotiations were in progress.'

Robin shook his head: 'No, that won't do. The anonym-ous caller gave a Chissingfield number, from which, as you know, there was no reply.'

'Doubtless, the call box where he was standing. He could hardly tell Verity it was urgent and then ring off leaving neither name nor number. And for the time being he had found out all he needed to know, which was that you were still here. The next step, you may be sure, was to try again as soon as he reached the cottage, but that turned out to be unnecessary. Bobbie told him we were on our way there and Tessa completed the business by kindly offering him the loan of your car. I rest my case.'

He was allowed to give it more rest than it deserved because before counsel for the defence, in the person of myself, could make mince meat of his accusations, we had been accosted by Mr Fellowes. He had evidently been sent on this errand by his wife, who I saw giving him a nod of encouragement, as he hovered within a yard of our table.

'Sorry if I'm interrupting anything, but Avril . . . we've been trying to attract your attention. We think it's high time we stood you that other half. What are you all drinking?'

When he had moved away to transmit the order to Kenneth, who had just been granted the rare opportunity to greet two customers from the outside world, Mrs Fellowes called out to ask what sort of a day we'd had. As there is no more uncomfortable way of conducting a conversation than across a distance of several yards, Robin pulled up two more chairs and invited her to join us.

'Terribly sweet of you,' she said, dropping into the nearer one. 'It seems silly to divide ourselves up when we're the only people here.'

'Although I see that two new passengers have come aboard,' I remarked. 'Whereas the others seem to have gone ashore for the evening. Or have they now abandoned ship?'

'No, I expect they'll be back soon. Denzil has taken them to see some play his son is performing in. He invited me and Charles to join them, but we've been feeling so cooped up that we decided to stick to our original plan and go for a good long tramp across the fields. It's some little theatre which no one round here has ever heard of, but I expect you know all about it, don't you, Tessa? I gather you and Jimmie are old friends?'

'Although I must say this is the first time I've heard of his father taking any interest in his career.'

'Frankly, I don't think he sees it as a suitable one for his son and heir, but I shall let you into a little secret. Oh, there you are, Charles! What an age! I thought you'd deserted us.'

'Yes, sorry about that, but Kenneth was in a talkative mood. He'll be over with our drinks in a minute.'

Familiar now with Mrs Fellowes's capacity for deviation and fearful of her little secret slipping from my grasp, I cued her in:

'You were saying something about Mr Godstow and Jimmie?'

'Oh yes, so I was. Well, you see, my dear, it's our belief that we have Diana's little friend, Stephanie, to thank for the expedition to the theatre this afternoon.'

'You mean she and Jimmie . . . ?'

'Exactly! Something in the wind there, unless I'm much mistaken. Didn't you notice the way she was yearning at him at Denzil's party?'

'Not specially. So many girls do spend half their time yearning at him that I've got used to it. I'm waiting for the day when he starts yearning back at one of them.'

'Well, my voices tell me that day may not be far off and let's hope they're right. She is just the kind of daughter-in-law Denzil would love to have and at least it would put an end to this silly feud.'

'Quite right!' Toby said. 'Two excellent reasons for a young man to enter into matrimony.'

'Oh dear, I must be careful what I say to you, mustn't I, Mr Crichton? You are much too cynical for romantic people like me. Really Charles, whatever can have happened to Kenneth? I suppose you did remember to tell him that we wanted the drinks now and not tomorrow morning?'

'Yes, he is taking his time, I'm afraid, but there's no rush, is there? We haven't got a train to catch.'

'All the same, I think you should go and have a tiny word with him.'

'Well, the fact is . . . he's had a bit of a knock, poor chap. Knock for me too, as it happens.'

'Oh dear, what was that?'

'Tell you later,' Charles said, in a sort of shamefaced rumble. 'Don't want to cast a blight over the proceedings.'

'My dear man, you are casting a blight, simply by sitting there and looking so stricken. Besides, if Kenneth knows, it will be all round the place in half an hour and I'm sure our friends would rather hear about it than be left wondering.'

As she was absolutely right, so far as at least one of their friends was concerned, I threw in some murmurs of encouragement and, still with obvious reluctance, he said:

'Well, fact is, those two chaps who just came in brought some rather bad news about an old friend of ours. It's poor Frank Winthrop, Avril.'

'No, really? What's happened to him?'

'Knocked down and killed, only a few hundred yards from his home, by one of those juggernauts. We always knew it would take a fatal accident to get something done about building a by-pass round Chissingfield and it had to be poor old Frank who's the human sacrifice.' From the corner of my eye I saw Robin's right hand move down to his pocket. He withdrew it again almost immediately, but I could not tell whether this was because he did not wish to study the telephone message until he was alone, or whether, as I considered more likely, he knew it by heart and had already realised that the number on it was the same as the one listed in his files under the name of Young Mr Winthrop.

(3)

'One way and another,' I said at dinner, which at our own request was late that evening, Robin having found it necessary to borrow Toby's car and disappear for half an hour, 'this has been a bad day. First Robin being frustrated over his telephone call and on top of that losing his brief case. Then poor Young Mr Winthrop and now this!'

The last was a reference to the fact that Mr God's party was once more in possession of the centre table, the numbers now somewhat depleted, but once again including Jimmie. Furthermore, he was seated next to Stephanie and making what I can only describe as much of her.

'You seem to have got your values mixed,' Robin said. 'Leaving aside the brief case, which may or may not turn out to be serious, I would hardly have bracketed the sudden death of an elderly and respected man with the sight of a young one making an ass of himself.'

'Particularly as I presume that you do not accept the idea that the sudden death was accidental?' Toby suggested.

'If so, it's a strange coincidence that he should have tried to get in touch with me only a few hours earlier. And it's not only we who know that, is it? Numerous people not a million miles from here could have known it too.'

'Well, Verity for a start,' I said, 'and she could have passed it on to Louisa or Jake, or both. Also Irene Gayford, who was by the desk when the call came through. Who else?'

'Absolutely all of them, as far as I can see, with the exception of Jimmie. Verity had stuck the message inside the Visitors' Book. In view of all the jostling around that went on this morning and the fact that she doesn't hesitate to leave the desk unattended whenever the whim takes her, she might just as well have pinned it up on the notice board.'

'On the other hand, I suppose there is just a chance that it was an accident? Everyone knows how these lorries go hurtling through towns and villages and you told me once that Young Mr Winthrop was going deaf. I don't suppose his hearing had improved since you last saw him.'

'Maybe not, but he doesn't appear to have gone blind as well, nor was there much hurtling this time. The driver insists that his speed was down to twenty miles an hour and, although it suits the pro by-pass brigade to discredit this, I personally do not.'

'Why?'

'Because it was Market Day, so not only was the middle of the road thronged with people, there was also a steady stream of pedestrians crossing back and forth. If he'd been going any faster, he'd have been in danger of mowing down half the population of Chissingfield. Also the road itself was jammed with cars, so if he was moving at a dangerous speed you have to accept that all the others were too.'

'How do you know all this? Did Kenneth tell you?'

'No, I got it from Superintendent Wilkins, who is in charge down here. An old acquaintance, I might add.'

'Don't tell me you've been to Chissingfield this evening? If so, you must have broken a few speed laws yourself.'

'No, only as far as the telephone kiosk, which, as you may have noticed, is beside the pillar box, almost opposite the gate. Past experience having made it imprudent to telephone him from here, it seemed the best way to let him know that his accident victim had been trying to get in touch with me.'

'And did you also tell him about your missing brief case?'

'Not yet. I may do so when I see him tomorrow.'

'What time tomorrow?'

'Eleven.'

'What about the races?'

'Oh, I expect to be through by then, but in any case there's no need for you two to hang around. I shall ask Anthony to bring my car here not later than ten thirty and he can go back with you. I tried to get hold of him just now, but of course he's out for dinner, so I'll have to leave it till the morning. Quite apart from the question of transport, I want to give it a more thorough going over than it probably got from him. I still think the brief case must be there somewhere, despite Toby's colourful theory.'

'And I suppose even he wouldn't dare suggest that Anthony was responsible for Young Mr Winthrop falling under a lorry, would you, Toby? You'd find it uphill work, considering he was sitting within yards of us when it happened.'

'I have never suggested that he was on his own, merely a vital cog in the machine. No doubt, one of his functions today was to equip himself with an unimpeachable alibi. That is why, when the doors of Mattingly Grange were closed to him, he hit on the idea of spending the day with Max and Bobbie. It was just as good.'

'And also quite a natural thing to have done, with the whole day ahead of him and nothing to fill it.'

'But why choose them? He is reputed to have dozens of friends down here, all with tastes and interests like his own. Why pick on people he hasn't seen for over a year? Could it be that because of that, they would carry more weight as witnesses?'

'More likely because he knew he could drop in on them at a moment's notice and be sure of a welcome. You might not be able to say the same of those other friends, however many interests they have in common. I really do think you're flogging a dead horse here.'

'And for once I agree with her,' Robin said.

'Then here is something else for you both to consider. How was it, do you suppose, that when you had taken such care to avoid a whisper getting out about Robin's job, the first question which Jake asked, when Tessa went calling on him in the summer house, was whether he had worked on the Chissingfield murder case?

Answer: someone had put it around that Scotland Yard were sending someone down here and who more likely to have done so than Anthony?'

Robin said: 'No, there is a simpler answer. It is just that, although the name conveyed nothing when I made the reservations, Jake did recognise me the instant he saw me in the dining room. I thought so at the time and I still do.'

'Then it was a fatuous question, was it not? If he had recognised you, it could only have been because of the murder case, so why ask?'

'Perhaps because he is not the devious character you take him for and did not realise that he was giving himself away.'

'And if you were to suggest that Jake had been a small cog in the machine,' I said, 'I should back you all the way. He was in the heart of Chissingfield at the time and ideally placed to see and hear what was going on. If he didn't know either Pauline or Young Mr Winthrop personally, he could certainly have picked up plenty of information about them and passed it on to interested parties.'

'But not directly involved?'

'He could have been. For example, did your Superintendent tell you what time the accident happened this afternoon, Robin?'

'Ten minutes past three.'

'There you are, that's just what I mean. For most men of his age it would be one of the most difficult times of all to be absent from their place of work, but not for Jake. In fact, the early part of the afternoon is when he is least in evidence and today was an absolute gift in that way. We were out to lunch and unlikely to return before five, the Fellowes had gone for a tramp and the Godstow party had booked seats for the theatre. He could have been asleep in his room, or patching up the summer house, or stalking a deaf old man until an opportune moment arrived to push him under a lorry.'

'Curiously enough,' Robin said, 'there is some evidence to suggest something of that kind happening. Wilkins told me of one witness who had the impression that there was someone with Winthrop when he fell. He couldn't give any description, except that he thought it was a young man.'

'So what more do you want?'

'Plenty. You don't need me to tell you that you can't charge someone with a crime simply because they're the right sex and had the opportunity to commit it. If that were all that could be said against him, I daresay it would leave a reasonable doubt in the minds of the jury.'

'The point is that it may not be all.'

'Your spies have told you that he was in Chissingfield this afternoon? I'm afraid it still wouldn't be damning enough. He probably always goes on Market Day.'

'No, this is something else. It is called the Tale of Two Picnics.'

I paused to allow this announcement to sink in, until Toby said:

'Well, don't overdo the pregnant silence.'

'It came to me just before we were interrupted by the Fellowes. The reason why Anthony couldn't find the brief case in the car was because it wasn't there and hadn't been there when we left the hotel this morning.'

'But I told you . . .' Robin began and then thought better of it.

'You told us that you had to move it to make room for the picnic baskets, but you'd got it mixed up, hadn't you? The picture in your mind belonged to the evening before, when we went to the theatre. You didn't open the boot at all this morning until we arrived at the cottage, because Verity had taken the keys so that Jake could see to it for you.'

'She's right, you know, Toby, I have to admit it.'

'So the only question is,' I went on, 'whether he arranged it like that on purpose, having failed to find anything of a confidential nature in our rooms, or whether he discovered the brief case by accident, and acted on impulse.'

'To be scrupulously fair, I suppose it is not quite the only question. It could have been Louisa who loaded up the car, or perhaps Verity shot off to do an investigation on her own, before handing over the keys.'

Toby said: 'And to be scrupulously fairer still, you would also need to ask yourselves whether whichever one it was acted on his own initiative or was merely obeying instructions.'

'What would the answer be, if you were writing it?'

'How can I say? Naturally, I should save it for the *dénouement.*'

'But you'd need to have worked it out in your mind by this time?'

'No, I regret to say that at this point I should probably be straightening pictures and waiting for an inspiration.'

I sighed: 'And it looks as though that is what we shall have to do, because we seem to be back where we started. We don't even know what has become of Robin's brief case.'

'Never mind, let us forget it for a while and turn our attention to the sub-plot, which now seems to be unfolding,' Toby said, looking up, as Jimmie approached our table. 'Unless, of course, he is a Greek messenger, bearing offers of brandy and liqueurs, in which case I'm off.'

(4)

'Good evening, Price, Mrs Price and cousin Toby Crich-ton.'

'Evening, Featherstone. How did it go this afternoon?'

'Not bad for a matinée, thank you. I had my claque there, which helped things along.'

'I should think it might have,' I said, 'seeing it probably accounted for twenty per cent of the audience. How's your wrist? I see you still have the bandage.'

'Yes, but that's just showing off. It doesn't hurt any more. Did Bobbie tell you I'd sprained it?'

'She mentioned it in passing.'

'And did she tell you how I did it?'

'She may have, I don't remember.'

'Ah well, I suppose I mustn't expect to dominate the conversation even in my absence. I came over to invite you . . .'

'Excuse me, will you?' Robin said, getting up, 'I must leave you for a few minutes. I have a phone call to make.'

'So must I,' Toby said, with equal alacrity, 'there is a picture in my room which badly needs straightening.'

'How very intuitive!' Jimmie said, watching them go. 'Whoever would have thought it?'

'I don't think either of them is feeling sociable this evening. It's been what they call a long day.'

'Well, it has saved me a lot of trouble. I can now throw away my script and speak from the heart.'

'What script?'

'Oh, just some rot about an argument I was having with our director about my interpretation of the part and want-ing your advice, ha ha. It would have sounded thin, even to them. I'm not a very brilliant liar, as you know, but since you now seem to be permanently flanked by those two gentlemen, the object was to prise you loose for half an hour and invite you to take a turn in the garden.'

'I shall be delighted.'

'Thank you, dear one. I rather think I do need your advice, you see, although not on the subject I had braced myself to rabbit on about.'

'Then we will go and sit in the summer house. The paint should be dry by now and it is just the place for confidences, especially of the romantic kind.'

'I must disillusion you, there is nothing romantic about this. Won't you need a coat?'

'I may, but I've left one in the car, so I can pick it up on my way out, if it's still there.'

'Why shouldn't it be?'

'Things have a way of disappearing in this place.'

This proved to be an understatement because when we arrived at the front door it was to discover that the car, as well as the coat inside it, had disappeared.

'Did they say where they were going?' I asked Louisa, who, by one of the minor miracles that occasionally broke the tedium of life at Mattingly Grange, was in charge of the desk and switchboard.

'No, just shot out without a word.'

'Well, if you see them, will you say I've gone for a moon-light stroll? Back in half an hour.'

'Will do. 'Fraid there's no moon tonight, though. Sorry about that.'

'Not your fault,' I assured her, 'and there's still some daylight left, which will do just as well. It was only a figure of speech.'

'Oh, I see! Jolly good! And, by the way, if you should happen to see Verity, you might tell her to pack it in now, will you?'

'Oh, certainly. Pack what in?'

'She's taken Lupus for a run.'

'Oh really? Another twilight walker?'

'You can say that again. She's been gone for hours and I could do with her here. I suppose the silly brute has run off and she can't get him back, but if you see her, tell her not to worry. She was stuck out there till nearly ten looking for him last night and we don't want any more of that. Next thing we know she'll be handing in her cards. Besides, he'll come home when he's ready to. He always does eventually.'

'Okay, we'll keep a look out for her.'

(5)

'I wonder if it was Lupus who kept her out so late last night?' I mused, as we strolled along past the stables.

'Why not?'

'No special reason. I was reminded of a drama I ran into soon after we arrived here. In the summer house too, curiously enough.'

'You're being very cryptic tonight, I must say. Oh, my God, is this it?' he asked, recoiling at the sight. 'It looks thoroughly unattractive and it'll be pitch dark inside, won't it? I should feel most uncomfortable listening to my own disembodied voice. Like doing a commercial from the tomb.'

'No need to go inside, we can sit on the steps. We'll be sheltered from the icy blast and screened from prying eyes by the rhododendrons.'

'Beastly, vulgar things,' he muttered gloomily, 'I loathe the sight of them. In fact, I loathe everything about this place and I wish I knew what it was that induced you to come here.'

'It's a long story and, since I gather you have one of your own to relate, it might be better to get that over first,' I said, seating myself on the middle step, with my feet on the bottom one.

It seemed at first that he had changed his mind, or else become so depressed by the surroundings as to have lost whatever urge he had once had to unburden himself, for he remained standing, with his back to me and head bent forward, as though staring at the ground. Then I saw the white strip gradually lengthening, as it dropped from his hand, and realised that he was unwinding the bandage. Finally, he bunched it into his right hand, seated himself beside my feet and placed his left arm across my knees.

'There you are, Miss Nightingale! Take a look at that!'

'It needs stitching,' I said, voicing the first thought that came into my head.

Spreading up his arm from the base of his thumb there was a pink gash, about four inches long and deep enough not to have closed up.

'You're probably right, but it won't be getting it. Bind it up again for me, will you? I have to use my teeth for the final stages.'

'Oughtn't it to have some disinfectant on first?'

'I'll see to that when I get home. Don't worry, I'm in no danger of neglecting myself.'

'You didn't get that by wrenching the steering wheel round,' I said, starting to re-wind the bandage.

'You're so right, my beloved.'

'And even if it eventually does heal up by itself, it'll be weeks before the scar fades. You can't go around for ever wearing a bandage and pretending you've sprained it.'

'Very true!'

'So if you know already why do you need to be told?'

'I don't need to be told. I am here to tell you something.'

'Okay, go ahead!'

'Are you sure you're not cold, Tessa?'

'I may survive, so long as we don't have to hang around all night, waiting for you to get to the point.'

'Very well, here we go! After that grisly birthday party, when I'd said goodnight to you lot, I drove to my father's house which, as you know, someone in his infinite wisdom has now seen fit to burn down.'

'Why?'

'Because he couldn't stand the sight of it any longer, I presume. And who shall blame him?'

'I meant, why did you go there?'

'That's not important.'

'Oh, come on, Jimmie, you know damn well it is. You don't get on with your father, you hate the house, so why the hell would you want to go there, late at night and on your own?'

'I was merely trying to stave off the pneumonia by sticking to essentials, but if you want every detail, so be it. It's true that I don't like my father. So much so that by the time I was fifteen I had managed to convince myself that he was not my father at all. I feel sure it was mutual. There have been numerous indications that he was able to reconcile himself to my contempt for all the values he holds dear by the belief that I was not his son. That is no longer the case, however. Or, if it is, he has forgiven my mother for the lapse. He is now showing a most unwelcome paternal interest.'

'Like in what way?'

'Like in inviting me to his ghastly birthday party. It was the last sort of gathering in which I should wish to be seen dead, but he had gone to the trouble of finding out that I wouldn't be on that evening and, as you know, I can never resist flattery, from whatever source. I told myself that it would be ungracious to refuse and Bobbie agreed. That doesn't mean much. She'd probably have agreed if I'd told her that I meant to take a gun to the party and shoot the birthday boy dead.'

'But you went and you didn't take a gun. Then what?'

'I wished I had, because during dinner he really went too far.'

'What did he do?'

'Started nagging me in front of the assembled company about going back to spend the night at Poltdean Towers. The name alone would put you off, wouldn't it?

I brought out every excuse in the book, except the true one, and he brushed them all aside, like the ash off his cigar, giving all the reasons, except the true one, why I should do as he asked.'

'What was the true one?'

'To get at Bobbie, of course. Make sure she had a sleepless night, imagining me lying dead in a ditch. Also one of the minor pleasures of his life is making a fool of me in public. He was succeeding so well that the only way to stop it was to give in to him.'

'I see!'

'Mind you, I hadn't the faintest intention of going. It was simply done to bring the ridiculous argument to an end. Then afterwards in the bar, when you finally managed to tear yourself away from his scintillating company, I made the excuse to see you up to your rooms, the plan being to jump in the car and drive with all speed to the cottage.'

'So why didn't you?'

'I suppose I'd had too much to drink, but halfway down the drive it struck me that by running away I should be playing straight into his hands. He'd be literally crowing with laughter and inviting all his creepy friends to share the joke.'

'I don't get it. What joke?'

'The one about the poor boy who'd gone slinking off into the night because otherwise he'd be in trouble with that fat, middle-aged shrew. Something on those lines, you can bet on it, and another of my weaknesses is that I can't bear being laughed at. So I decided that the last laugh should be mine. I'd let him have his fun and then, when they all arrived home, there I'd be, waiting for them. I'd get out of the car and say: "Oh, my goodness, I thought you were never coming! Never mind, who's for a game of bridge before we go to bed?" Very childish, I know, but I'm afraid he does bring out the infantile side in my character.'

'So what went wrong? Something, obviously?'

'The word is everything. It started before I reached the house. There's a two-mile drive up to the front door, which is quite in keeping with all its other pretensions, but I didn't go that way. It's quicker if you're driving from here to take a side turning at Mattingly Bottom, which leads to what used to be the barns and midden of the home farm. They're scheduled buildings and so, for all his attempts at bribery and corruption, he wasn't allowed to tear them down and put up an ornamental aviary. He cut his losses and handed them over to the National Trust, but there's still a footpath from there up to the side of the house; only when I got to the turning to the barns I found my entry blocked by a van facing towards the lane. I damn near crashed into it too because there were no lights on and it was pitch dark under the trees.'

'What did you do?'

'What I should have done, if I'd had my wits about me, was to turn round and drive straight back to my own wee home, but my blood was up by then and I was not to be put off.'

'And another thing you could have done, I suppose, was to drive straight to the nearest telephone and report it?'

'Yes, that might not have been such a bad idea either, but I can't have been thinking very clearly. It did flit through my mind that whoever had left the van there was probably up to no good, but that was all. I didn't follow it through and, instead of doing either of those sensible things, I parked my car on the grass at the edge of the lane, squeezed my way past the van and went tripping up towards the footpath.'

'Straight into the welcoming arms of the fire-raisers?'

'No, what I am appalled to realise is that I most likely missed those welcoming arms by a couple of seconds. They must have been crouched down inside the van. I hadn't gone more than fifty yards before I heard the engine start up and when I looked back the van was turning into the lane. I suppose they'd finished the job and were about to take off when they saw me coming. The lane's dead straight up to that point, so they'd have had ample time to conceal themselves. I imagine they just sat there, with their fingers crossed, waiting for me to go by.'

'Where to?'

'The farmhouse is just a bit further on. It's a run-down old place now and I expect the farmer and his wife are in bed and asleep by ten o'clock most nights of the week, but it must have seemed a more likely place for me to be making for than the barns. Very few people, apart from my father, know about the footpath and he would never dream of using it.'

'All the same, it's funny that they didn't try and head you off, either by force, or gentle persuasion.'

'Except that, for all they knew, there could have been several of us in the car. In which case, if the others had seen me being attacked they wouldn't just have looked on in horror and amazement. At the very least, they'd have bolted back to the village and alerted the police. My guess is, though, that they didn't stop to reason why, just did what came naturally and ducked out of sight, hoping to make a dash for it as soon as I'd gone by.'

'And was the house on fire when you got there?'

'Oh, yes. You couldn't have told from a distance because there were no flames leaping around, but when I closed in

I could see smoke filtering out from the first floor gallery, where he keeps all his treasures.'

'So what did you do?'

'Behaved like a raving lunatic is the answer. If I'd been my normal self, nothing would have pleased me better than the sight of that hideous edifice going up in flames. On the rare occasions when I go there I'm always tempted to put a match to it myself, but I was too wound up by then to behave rationally. Faced with this crisis and without a living soul within hailing distance, I found myself flinging off the mantle of cynicism, which it has taken me all these years to stitch together, and plunging into the fray.'

'And where did that land you?'

'Covered with blood, if you really wanted to know. I knew the front door would be bolted and barred, so I looked around for some other way to get in. The idea being, you understand, simply to fight my way to a telephone to alert the Fire Brigade and that was all. I hadn't sunk so low as to entertain ideas about waiting for them, or trying to put the fire out single-handed. How to proceed, though, was quite a problem. One of the worst excrescences which my father perpetrated when he bought the house was to have all the ground floor windows removed and replaced by those hideous leaded panes. I tried to explain to him that the only reason why the Tudors put up with them was because they hadn't learnt any better, but he took no notice.'

'There are people who believe them to be quite effective burglar deterrents.'

'Then they delude themselves. One of the panes, slap in the middle of the pantry window, was a gaping hole. All I had to do was stick my hand through, lift the catch, stage left, and hey presto! Or very nearly presto. Unfortunately, I was without my do-it-yourself burglar kit, otherwise I might have been wearing protective clothing. Another disadvantage was that I'd failed to notice how jagged the glass was round the edges. The result you have now seen.'

'So what was the next move?'

'Short of remaining there until I expired from loss of blood, there was only one thing I could do. I took off my jacket and shirt, wrapped the shirt round my wrist, slung the jacket over my shoulders and beat it back to the car. I was all right then, because I do carry a First Aid box with me. That's one of Bobbie's little precautions. God knows why, but she's convinced that one day the windscreen will splinter and my box office face will be slashed to ribbons. Anyway, it came in handy last night.'

'So then you drove home and went to bed and the next morning you told her you had sprained your wrist? Why?'

'Pretty feeble, I agree, but it was the best I could think of.'

'But why not the truth?'

'Because she wouldn't have believed me. I could hardly believe it myself when I woke up. The whole episode seemed so utterly wild and dream-like. I wanted to put it out of my mind and pretend it really had been a dream. If she had believed me, she'd have concluded I was drunk, and that was the last sort of complication I needed. So I told her the first lie that came into my head.'

'I'm not sure that she believed that either, as a matter of fact.'

'Maybe not, but at least she hasn't kept on at me about it. Although I can't see that blessed relief lasting much longer.'

'Neither can I.'

'If I'd realised how deep the cut was, I'd have spent more time working out my story, but I was expecting it to heal up in a couple of days, at which point I'd be able to get by with a little clever make-up.'

'So what do you want me to do? Help you concoct a better story?'

'Oh, no, there'd be no point in that. If it comes to the worst, I'll have to tell her the shaming truth, but what I want from you is something only you, with your inside knowledge, might know.'

'What's that?'

'What attitude will the police take and what should my response be when they discover that I was at the Towers last night, standing on the very same spot where the break-in was made?'

'But why should they, Jimmie? I realise that there would be blood and finger prints on the window frame and maybe footprints as well, but they'd have no reason to compare them with yours.'

'Not yet, but the time is bound to come when they do.'

'I don't see why . . . unless . . . could there be more to this story than you've told me?'

'Just the postscript. When I'd disinfected the cut and bound it up, I rolled up my shirt and threw it into the bushes.'

'Oh, dear!'

'Yes, no need to tell me how dim-witted that was. I can see it for myself now, but at the time I was concentrating on Bobbie. The jacket was no great problem because I knew I could hang it in my cupboard until the opportune moment arrived for taking it to the cleaners, but a bloodstained shirt is not an easy article to dispose of in a four-room rented cottage.'

'No.'

'Obviously, it's not the kind of thing the bloodhounds will be looking for, but, barring a miracle, someone, someday is sure to find it and most likely take it to the police and I can see that landing me in some tedious explanations. That's why I need your advice and one reason why I allowed myself to be dragged into another of these macabre *soirées*. The other was to revisit the scene of the crime. I went there, on

my way here, to see if I could retrieve the shirt, but everything looked so different in the daylight and I realised that I
might be searching around in those woods for hours before
I found it. Furthermore, I had the uneasy feeling that someone was watching me. That may have been imagination, but
it occurred to me that I hadn't done myself much good by
giving way to the impulse of the moment and the time had
come to play it cautious. So tell me this, if you will, Tessa;
are the police now patrolling the grounds and, if they were
to catch me creeping around in the vicinity, am I likely to
be arrested for arson, if not worse?'

'I wouldn't have thought so, but you shouldn't take my
word for it. Robin might know what they're up to, or at any
rate he could find out. With your permission, I suggest we
now set forth and, if he's back, repeat everything you've
told me. Apart from your own troubles, I'm getting stiff
with cold.'

Having sought my advice and been given it in generous
doses, I was rather put out to see that he appeared not to be
listening. His mouth had dropped open and he was staring
into the middle distance with a glazed expression.

'My God, Tessa, did you see that, or have I gone right
off my head?'

'See what?'

'That thing . . . animal, that just went streaking up the
garden. It had yellow eyes and it looked like a wolf.'

'Oh, that was only Lupus. He is a sort of wolf, but quite
harmless, so they tell me, so long as you don't put your hand
out. I suppose he escaped again and Verity is now scouring
the countryside. She will not be pleased. Did you hear what
I said? I think we should now go and find Robin. If I still
have the use of my limbs, that is.'

'What's the matter with your limbs?'

'They've gone stiff with cold.'

'Oh yes, so you said. Sorry about that. Shall I see if there's a rug in there that you could wrap yourself into for the walk home?'

'Don't bother, I expect I'll manage.'

Ignoring this, he got up and walked past me into the summer house. Several minutes went by before he came out again and I used the time by getting the circulation going with some bending and stretching exercises. I was standing on the grass at the bottom of the steps, with my hands raised above my head, when he appeared in the doorway. The pair of us would have presented a curious spectacle for any observer, for he remained motionless and silent as Lot's wife, with an expression on his face to match, which temporarily froze me into immobility as well.

'Did you find anything?' I asked, dropping my arms.

'No. Yes.'

'Which do you mean and why are you looking like that? Are you ill?'

'Yes. There's a woman in there, lying on the floor. She must have been there the whole time we were talking.'

'Yes, I suppose she was, and what's she doing on the floor?'

'I don't know. I almost fell on top of her. The most hideous moment of my life. I couldn't see much and I didn't want to touch her, but there was something . . . I think she's dead, Tessa. In fact, I'm certain of it.'

(6)

Several years later, or so it seemed, Robin and Toby and I were assembled in the bar, where the management had laid on hot soup for those of its battered guests who still had the energy to consume it.

Kenneth was in charge, a tight lipped Louisa having strode in and out again at one point, to apologise for the inconvenience resulting from the death of her receptionist, and the Fellowes had also now drifted away.

The members of the Godstow contingent had retired to their own apartments at the conclusion of their brief and separate interviews with Superintendent Wilkins, and Jimmie, who had been called first and detained longest, was now on his way home to the comforting arms of Roberta.

On our side, Toby had been required merely to state his name, address and purpose of visit and my own ordeal had lasted scarcely longer. Robin had been third on their list and he had not come out again until two hours later, when these preliminary enquiries were over, having been invited to remain as an observer.

'And what did you observe?' I asked him.

'Don't you think we should pack it in now and go to bed, while we still have the strength to crawl upstairs?'

'Oh no, I could never sleep in my present state of suspense. Nor could you, Toby, could you?'

'Perhaps not. Or perhaps I no longer have the strength to crawl upstairs. It would be less trouble to sit here until I fall asleep in my chair.'

'There is not much to tell,' Robin said, then turned to address Kenneth:

'Don't stay unless you have to. We shan't be needing anything else.'

'Very good, squire. If you say so, I'll be off home and get some kip,' he replied, too exhausted now to grapple with a foreign tongue.

'The first thing to know,' I said, 'is how and when she was killed.'

'We'll have to wait for the post mortem to confirm it, but the police surgeon reckoned she'd been dead for between two-and-a-half and three hours when he saw her. She appears to have been strangled by someone standing behind her, wearing gloves. There was a pair of those cotton dusting gloves, with elasticated cuffs, lying on the floor.'

'Jimmie and I must have got there around nine and we were talking for twenty minutes or so before he went into the summer house. Allow another half hour before the police took over and what does that give us? I can't work it out.'

'Seven to seven-thirty, near enough. Highly inconvenient time for checking alibis, as you may imagine. Needless to say, they all had plausible tales to relate, to cover the period from six-thirty onwards.'

'What do they claim to have been doing? Don't go to sleep just yet, Toby, this is getting interesting.'

'Jake was in the kitchen, putting the finishing touches to the dinner. Louisa, for what it's worth, says she went in there several times, either to give him a hand, or pass on something he ought to know about numbers in the dining room and so on. But the fact is that, with or without her knowledge, he could have been absent for up to ten or fifteen minutes. There's a door between the kitchen and back staircase, opening on to the garden at the side of the house, and a path leading to the stables.'

'Does he really cope with all the cooking on his own? No kitchen staff at all?'

'If so,' Toby remarked, 'I shall have a word to say on the subject to Mrs Parkes next time she complains about only having one pair of hands.'

'He does have some help, but only on a rota basis. There are two local women who each come three days a week. Their job is mainly cleaning, preparing vegetables and so on. They leave between two and three in the afternoon, depending on the amount of washing up after lunch. The two waitresses, who live in the flat over the stables, come on duty at midday till around three o'clock and again at seven-thirty in the evening. Finally, there's a youthful moonlighter, who's supposed to come at nine to wash up after dinner, but he's not very reliable and sometimes, on a busy evening, Jake and Louisa are hard at it until after midnight. When you remember that they have to be back in the kitchen to start on the breakfast trays soon after seven, it's not surprising that they have a tendency to disappear during the afternoon. About the only time they get to clean out the stables and dig the garden. However, the point is that between approximately six o'clock and seven-thirty Jake is virtually on his own.'

'Which also applies to Louisa, presumably?'

'Not to the same extent because she and Verity were more or less interchangeable during the late afternoon and evening, taking over from each other, or more often not, as the need arose. Obviously, there were lulls when she could have nipped out, but it would have needed timing and luck to have hit on the right one. She was certainly on duty at the desk when the Godstow lot returned from the theatre and again between seven and half past when the Fellowes came down and went into the bar. She was still there when Jimmie turned up soon afterwards.'

'And there's another reason why Louisa doesn't qualify,' I said. 'Whoever killed Verity must surely have arranged to meet her at a certain time in the summer house and it's hard to imagine what excuse Louisa could have found for that. If they had anything to say to each other, there was nothing to prevent their saying it indoors. Jake is a much more promising candidate in that respect.'

'You have missed the point,' Toby told me.

'Oh, have I? What point?'

'In assuming that the one who made the appointment with Verity was also the murderer. If Louisa had overheard the other two planning an assignation, she could have gone to the kitchen ten minutes before the appointed time, flung out some excuse to keep Jake chained to the stove and set off at a brisk pace for the summer house. If Jake had turned up later and found Verity dead, he would have been in no great hurry to advertise the fact.'

'You're both going too fast,' Robin said. 'For the moment all we're concerned about is who could or could not have been in the summer house during the relevant period. It turns out that Jake and Louisa both could, although it would have been that much easier for him. Unfortunately, that doesn't make him unique. In fact, the only one who appears to be entirely in the clear is Kenneth. His story is that he opened up the bar at six o'clock, as he does every evening, and that he remained there until closing time. There seems no reason to disbelieve him. Since it's open to non-residents as well, he is the one person whose absence, even for five minutes, would have been noticed. Besides, I agree with Tessa that in all probability it was the murderer who arranged to meet Verity and it is hard to see why Kenneth should have chosen such a time for it.'

'All right,' I said, 'so now tell us about the others. Starting with the Fellowes.'

'It wouldn't matter where I started. In essence, each story is much like another. The only variation is in the details.'

'Then you had better give us the details,' Toby said, 'and let us see what we can do with those.'

'In chronological order, it goes like this: the Fellowes returned from their walk soon after five and went to their room. They asked for tea, which was taken up to them by Verity. Avril then lay down for an hour, while Charles wrote some letters. At six-fifteen, he came downstairs, with the letters in his hand, saying that he was taking them to the pillar box.'

'The last post would have gone by then,' I said.

'As Verity pointed out to him, but he explained that he wanted to be sure of their catching the first collection in the morning. She wasn't there, and neither was Louisa when he got back, but he and his wife came down together about an hour later. Between those two appearances, Godstow had returned with his daughter and Stephanie and they too had gone to their rooms to bath and change, Godstow in one and the two girls together in another. Unlike the Fellowes, they came down one at a time. Diana was the first and she went out to the terrace, having ordered a drink which was brought to her by Kenneth. Stephanie followed about twenty minutes later and Louisa, who by then had taken over the desk, told her where to find Diana. They were eventually joined by Mr God, who stopped on his way through to ask whether his son had arrived, to which Louisa replied that she had not seen him, but she had been out in the kitchen for the past five or ten minutes. All these stories have been corroborated to some extent and they bring us, by a natural sequence, to Jimmie, who has produced the only one so far to arouse more than a spark of interest.'

'How can you say that,' I protested, 'when clearly every-one you've mentioned had a perfect opportunity to go to the summer house, by way of the back staircase, without the others knowing?'

'Yes, but they'd have needed luck to time it right. That almost rules out Godstow, incidentally, doesn't it? Also there appears to be no hint of a motive for any of them. However, that is another kettle of fish, which is nowhere near coming to the boil yet and, in the meantime, Jimmie's story does contain a couple of discrepancies which may need following up. Well?'

'Well, what?'

'Why aren't you jumping about and declaring him to be innocent, long before you've heard what they are?'

'I think I can guess what one of them is, but go on!'

'The curtain came down at ten past five. No one went round to see him afterwards, but there was a note from his father at the stage door, inviting him to join them here for dinner. As a result, when he had changed and taken off his make-up, he went to the phone box in the foyer and rang Bobbie to tell her that he would not be home till late. Wilkins, understandably, accepted that as perfectly normal behaviour, but I confess I was surprised.'

'Why?'

'Well, honestly, Tessa, aren't you the one who's always going on about how he can hardly bring himself to speak to his father? And now here he is, accepting two invitations from him in a week. So what's happened?'

'I can tell you exactly what's happened,' Toby said. 'Love has conquered. I cannot say I admire his taste, but we all saw him gazing into her eyes and laughing at her silly jokes this evening.'

'Yes, we did and, personally, I thought he was laying it on a bit too thick. I could be wrong, but it struck me that there was something phoney about it. For one thing, I don't recall his paying any special attention to her at the birthday party and, in fact, he walked out without saying goodnight to her. Furthermore, as soon as he'd swallowed his dinner this evening he marched up to invite Tessa to accompany him on a moonlight walk. That doesn't sound very lover-like behaviour to me. Unless, the object of this exercise was to reveal the secrets of his heart and maybe seek some practical advice on a tactful way of breaking the news to Roberta?'

'No,' I admitted, 'so far as I remember, the subject of Stephanie was not mentioned,' and then, unsure whether in these new circumstances the time had yet come, or would ever come, to talk about bloodstained shirts concealed in bushes, I left it there and said: 'Well, come on, tell us about the other discrepancy!'

Robin gave me a speculative look, as of one registering a point for inclusion in the files, and then continued: 'It concerns the more practical matter of the time element. As I told you, the curtain was down at ten past five and so, as he admits, allowing for the time it took him to change and make the telephone call, he was ready to leave, and doubtless was seen to do so, by six o'clock. He arrived here at seven-forty. In other words, it took him just over an hour and a half to cover a distance of thirty miles.'

I had been prepared for this and I said: 'Don't forget his wrist. He was probably hampered by that and taking it extra slow.'

'No, we have not been allowed to forget it. He drew our attention to it, when the time gap was pointed out to him.'

'And it is true, you know, Robin. He told me how it happened. It had nothing to do with this evening's events, so I needn't go into it now, but I promise you he's not faking.'

'Maybe not, but you can tell by the way he uses it, when he's concentrating on something else, that it doesn't inconvenience him all that much. Certainly not enough to add thirty or forty minutes to the journey and, in fact, there are grounds for believing that he arrived here at least half an hour earlier than he says.'

'What grounds?'

'Someone else is almost certain of having seen him near the main gate before seven o'clock.'

'Who?'

'Charles Fellowes, on his way back from the pillar box. He stopped at the end of the drive because there was a car coming up on his right. It was going slowly and the left hand indicator was flashing, but he has little faith in his fellow motorists, so he waited to make sure, which was just as well.

At the last minute the driver changed his mind, picked up speed and drove on past. So, one way and another, Fellowes had plenty of time to observe the car and he still thinks it was Featherstone's.'

'Why still?'

'In the sense that he did not question it at the time and the element of doubt crept in later. The impression we got was that it was not so much doubt as embarrassment that made him hesitate. He had realised by then what his evidence could imply.'

'And there is also an outside chance, is there not, that he invented the evidence? That what he actually did when he walked out of the hotel, brandishing his letters, was to stuff them in his pocket and streak off to the summer house. It's only his word against Jimmie's.'

'Quite so, but I have to tell you that, of the two words, his is the one which Wilkins is more inclined to accept. You may put that down to prejudice on his part, but you have to admit that there's no reason on earth why Fellowes should have made it up. It does nothing to substantiate his own story and he cannot be so simple as to imagine that it provides him with anything resembling an alibi.'

'So what happens next?'

'Nothing, for the moment, and perhaps nothing in the future, either, unless some more positive evidence were to turn up. For the time being, it remains as just a question mark against his name. And so . . .'

'So what?'

'If you were to be invited out for another walk in the garden, it might be a friendly gesture to advise him to dream up a slightly more convincing way to account for those missing forty minutes.'

DAY FIVE

(1)

THERE were twenty-three runners listed in the morning paper for the fifth race, which was at four o'clock. It was an amateur maiden chase and one of them, Pagan Lad by name, was owned, trained and ridden by Mr Anthony Blewiston. Another was called Flight Path, trained by Jock Symington and ridden by Mrs Louisa Coote.

'I had no idea you were in that league,' I told her, putting the newspaper down, as she wheeled in the breakfast trolley. 'Are you nervous?'

'Not specially. Too much on my mind for that.'

'Yes, I'm sure. I wonder that you feel able to go through with it?'

'Oh well, I did think of backing out, but what would be the use of that? It wouldn't do Verity any good and I'd feel worse than ever letting Jock down. He'd have a hell of a job finding another rider at such short notice and he can't scratch now, without losing money.'

This made sense, but I wondered if she might also be using the occasion to demonstrate to the world that, despite everything, no cloud of suspicion was hanging over Mattingly Grange.

'Shall we put our money on you?' I asked.

'Shouldn't, if I were you. He's a game little chap, but he'll be up against some stiff competition today and that rain we had the other night won't have pleased him. Also he likes to be up there in front, right from the start and, with such a large field, that won't be easy.'

The tight-lipped expression was relaxing now, so before she could command us to let us know if there was anything we needed, I took a chance and asked whether there had been any news from the police.

'Not a word, but I don't suppose we'll be left in peace for long.'

'I thought they might be here already. I saw one of their cars outside.'

'Oh, that was just the relief man, taking over guard duty at the summer house. There's been one poor bloke out there all night, I can't imagine why. Anyone would think they expected the murderer to come creeping back to see if he'd left his hat and gloves behind.'

'Stranger things have happened,' Robin remarked, 'Although, if anyone had done that, Tessa would probably have taken it as proof of his innocence.'

'Too true!' I agreed, thinking of Jimmie and his blood-stained shirt. 'Tell us about Verity, though. Had you known her long?'

'No, never set eyes on her until a few months ago, when she came for the interview.'

'For the job?'

'Yes, we'd advertised for a receptionist. Not a permanency, just for the season. We got quite a stack of answers, as a matter of fact, but most of the applicants were students, looking for free board and lodging during the summer vacation. That wasn't any use to us and you could tell straight off that they weren't a scrap interested in the job. Verity was the only one who showed the right attitude. She'd had no training, but she was willing to take on any old job that came up. She had the right sort of background too. You know, used to horses and knew how to talk to people and all that.'

'Did she have any family?'

'Of a sort. They're obviously well heeled, but they didn't have much time for her. She was brought up by nannies and governesses and what not. Then, when she was about twelve, her parents divorced and she was packed off to some posh boarding school. Two or three years later they both re-married and her mother went to live in Canada. By the time Verity was grown up she'd acquired quite a collection of half brothers and sisters, so she'd always been odd man out.'

'But she still had part of her family in this country? Do they live anywhere near?'

'Oh Lord, no, Yorkshire. That was the first thing the police wanted to know and luckily I'd kept the letter she wrote when she applied for the job, so I was able to give them her father's address.'

'So why did she choose to come and work down here? Was it simply because it was so far from Yorkshire?'

'I think one reason was because quite often, during the school holidays, she'd been shunted off to stay with her grandmother in Bath. All that came to an end two or three years ago, when the grandmother died, but Verity told me once that those visits were the happiest times of her life and she'd made one or two friends there. So I suppose that was the attraction. And now I'd better get a move on, if you've got everything you need?'

'Yes, of course, you must have a hell of a lot to do?'

'Oh, it's not so bad. All our lot will be at the races and we're closed to non-residents until further notice, so no lunch to worry about. Still, there's always plenty to see to in this job, so I must press on. If I don't see you, have a good day!'

'It's curious, isn't it,' I said to Robin, 'how this phrase "two or three years" keeps cropping up? Had you noticed?'

'Not particularly. I know of one incident that occurred two or three years ago and it's been haunting us ever since we arrived here. Have there been others?'

'Several. Jake said it was two or three years ago that he and Louisa branched out and took over Mattingly Grange. And Toby, as you'll recall, reminded us that it was two or three years ago that Anthony inherited his money. It must have been at about the same time as the Fellowes retired and now we hear that two or three years ago Verity stopped coming to Bath. I don't suppose it means anything, but the coincidence keeps piling up and the annoying thing is that I have a vague recollection of someone else using the same phrase, in yet another context, only I can't remember who it was.'

'I suppose we've been led down so many new paths during this so-called holiday that it's difficult to keep track of them all. Yesterday you were getting steamed up over whatever it was you ought to have remembered about the pub where Anthony's staying.'

'The Weston Arms. No, that's ceased to be a problem. I have remembered.'

'So at least you've got that one tidied up and in its right place?'

'Well, not entirely and the reason I haven't referred to it before is that I didn't want it to get to Toby's ears.'

'Whyever not?'

'It puts another black mark against Anthony. The Weston Arms used to belong to Jake and Louisa. Jake mentioned it only a few hours after we arrived here and he told me it was where they first started to build up their reputation for gourmet food. They sold it, two or three years ago, don't forget, in order to move up the ladder to this place. So, if Anthony chose it out of all the others he could have stayed in, the chances are that he knew it in their day and could well have been there during the race meeting which coincided with Pauline's murder. How about that?'

'Nothing whatever about that. He most certainly was not there. Admittedly, if he had been, he'd have left long before I arrived, but you seem to have no conception of how painstaking and laborious that investigation was. Every single hotel register for miles around came under scrutiny and, if Anthony's name had been there, I should have recognised it at once.'

'Yes, I'm sure you would, but what's the use of that? You know how careless the Cootes are about such formalities? The first thing Louisa impressed on you when we arrived was that there was no hurry about signing in.'

'Nevertheless, I did sign and I bet, if I hadn't done so within twenty-four hours, she'd have reminded me. That casual sort of attitude is just part of the act, designed to make the new arrivals feel they are members of some grand private house party. It wouldn't have held up for long. No sane hotelier could afford to bend the rules to that extent.'

'On the other hand, I can easily believe that, if Anthony had told them that he was running away from his creditors or some jealous female and wanted to register under a false name, they wouldn't have turned a hair. If any questions had come up later, which at that time must have seemed highly unlikely, they could always claim that they had no idea that his name wasn't John Smith.'

'Well, you have a point there, I must admit.'

'Though I don't know why I have gone to all this trouble to make it. I simply set out to explain why I'd been in no hurry to pass the news on to Toby.'

'And I'm afraid you've succeeded all too well. I still think his theory is a load of rubbish, but I'm clutching at straws now and I'm not sure it wouldn't be worth while getting Wetherbys to turn up their records for that meeting.'

'What for?'

'To provide us with a list of the owners and trainers who'd entered for it.'

'I wouldn't bother, if I were you.'

'It wouldn't be much bother.'

'All the same, I think you'd be wasting your time.'

'Why? Apart, that is, from interfering with your laudable efforts to spare your old friend the embarrassment of having to answer a few questions?'

'Three reasons, really. The first being that he is my old friend.'

'And therefore above suspicion?'

'Exactly! I may not have a very scientific approach to life, but neither do I consider myself to be moronically unobservant and, if Anthony possessed a murderous, or even conspiracy to murderous streak, I should have noticed signs of it before. The second is that eventually I shall remember who it was who told me of another event which took place two or three years ago and, when I do, it may add a new dimension to the picture.'

'Well, don't forget to let me know about it. What's the third?'

'Oh, that's even less scientific, so you won't be surprised to hear it's the one I set most store by. I have a hunch that I already know who murdered Pauline and Verity.'

(2)

The one I did not believe to be the murderer was waiting in the hall when I went downstairs at ten o'clock. With a punctiliousness, as he would no doubt have put it, above and beyond the call of duty, he had brought Robin's car back half an hour before the appointed time, although curiosity may have had something to do with it too.

'Did they let you through without any harassment?' I asked him.

'Oh yes, no bother at all. Didn't even search me for firearms. I suppose Robin had prepared the ground. Bit of luck for them, wasn't it, having him here on the spot when the murder was committed?'

'It didn't prevent its happening.'

'No, but since it has, it must be a fine thing to be able to hand it over to the expert.'

'Oh no, Anthony, that's not at all the way such things are arranged. If they wanted help from Scotland Yard, they'd have to apply for it and admit they weren't competent to handle the case on their own, which no one is ever particularly eager to do. Then, if someone from outside did take over, it wouldn't necessarily be Robin. He is supposed to be on leave, after all. They might put someone quite different in charge.'

'More fools them! And a shocking waste of the taxpayers' money, in my opinion.'

'Don't be silly, there are dozens of Chief Inspectors just as experienced as Robin.'

'My point is that none of the others have the advantage of knowing the background like he does. All those weeks he was here on that other case and, if it should turn out that there's some connection between that and this new one, well, he'd have a head start, wouldn't he? No denying that.'

'I'm not denying it, Anthony, I just can't make out why you think there might be a connection. No one else has suggested such a thing.'

'Yes, they have.'

'Who?'

'Some of the locals in that pub where I'm stopping.'

'The Weston Arms?'

'That's right. They were full of it. They'd been talking earlier about some old chap who'd been run over and killed in the market place and one of them remembered that the girl in the race course murder had been his secretary. The consensus was that it was a funny coincidence and no mistake. Then someone else came in just before closing time with the news that another young lady had been done in up at Mattingly and that fairly clinched the matter. You'd have a job convincing them there's no connection.'

'I expect I would, but how the hell could the news have spread so quickly? I know for a fact that the police weren't called in till after nine and those places have to close at ten, don't they?'

'Ten thirty, and it just goes to show what a town girl you are, Tessa, if you imagine that an hour and a half isn't ample time for news of that sort to be passed around among the drinking public. Matter of fact, though, to be fair, they did get a little help from one of their friends on this occasion.'

'Not you, by any chance?'

'Oh Lord, no, not me. What would I know, when I'd spent the whole evening there, chatting to the bumpkins? No, this was our local reporter, fellow named Rogerson. He writes the sports page, among other literary flights, so I've had occasion to run into him from time to time. Anyway, he'd been round to the police station, making his routine check on the latest Chissingfield crime figures, what the teenage burglars had been up to and so forth, but he'd hardly got started on it when the desk sergeant had to break it up to take a phone call. After that there wasn't a hope of getting anyone to pay any attention to him. They were all charging about like Keystone Kops and they more or less told him to move along there, please, so he knew it was something big and, after they'd all gone zooming off, with sirens screaming, he managed, by what means we do not enquire, to get the outline from one of the underlings who'd been left behind.'

'At which point I'd have expected him to hurry round to his office and start typing it up for his editor.'

'Well, you couldn't exactly call it a scoop, dear heart. His paper won't be printed again till next Thursday and the story will have lost some of its edge by then. Knowing him, I imagine the first move was to ring up some other trusty contact on a London newspaper and then, with ten minutes to go before closing time, what better than to whip up a little local honour and glory by nipping round the corner to the Weston Arms. And that's the story of how I come to be so well informed.'

And I had no doubt that, in general, it was a truthful one, despite one statement it contained being somewhat at variance with the facts and, to draw him out further, I said:

'And they all concluded it was tied up in some way with the other murder? I still don't understand why. I see the connection between the first girl and the old man, but surely that's where it ends? I don't suppose either of them knew of Verity's existence.'

'Ah, but what it indicated to my friends in the saloon bar was that the murderer is now back with us and up to his old tricks again.'

'Making it necessary for him to start by eliminating Mr Winthrop, who would be in a position, when the second murder was committed, to step forward and say "There is Your Man!"?'

'That was precisely their deduction.'

'On the assumption, of course, that he is not a local man?'

'As they have believed all along, although now seeing him as a somewhat special outsider.'

'He would have to be that, I suppose. Special in what way?'

'A racing man, for one thing. They attach great significance to the fact that both these murders occurred on the eve of a big race.'

'Yes, that's true. Any other similarities?'

'Oh yes, amateur detectives to a man, this bunch. They were quick to see that, although both young ladies were living in the neighbourhood at the time, it was for reasons of employment, rather than natural causes, as it were. They were outsiders themselves, in a sense.'

'You seem to have covered quite a lot of ground in ten minutes.'

'Ah well, you see, the landlord allows himself to be a little flexible in these matters, especially when the police force is known to be heavily engaged elsewhere. At one point, I recall, we adjourned to his private apartments at the back of the house and he plied his trade from there.'

'It must have been a profitable evening. Does he serve food, as well?'

'No, only the old sausage roll and hunk of bread and cheese. In any case, no one felt hungry for the real thing, with all that food for thought being dished out.'

'I was wondering how you'd managed about dinner?' There was a moment's uncomfortable silence. It lasted no longer than that and on my side was tinged with relief that Toby was not present to witness the effect of my booby trap. It could only have added fuel to his flames, for I saw that Anthony now wore the expression which I would have expected him to reserve for the stable lad who had been caught stirring tranquillisers into the bran mash. This, too, passed off quickly and he said in his normal good humoured voice:

'The landlord's wife knocked me up an omelette, as a special favour. It wasn't very good, but there's no such thing as a decent restaurant in Chissingfield and I didn't need much after that whacking great picnic you laid on for us at the cottage.'

'Well, that was Mattingly Grange at its peak. Did you ever meet Verity, by the way?'

'Verity?'

'The receptionist, the one who's been murdered.'

'Oh, was that her name? No, I didn't. I don't think she'd joined the ranks last time I was here.'

'Or the other one either, I suppose? Pauline?'

'Yes, curiously enough, I think I may have met her on one occasion. I'd either forgotten, or never knew her name, so it meant nothing to me when she was killed, but last night, when they were all hammering away at it and they mentioned she'd been secretary to this man, Winthrop, I realised she must have been the one.'

'Which one?'

'That I met when I was up here a couple of years ago. An aunt of mine had died and left me some money. I'd always known I'd come into it eventually, but it was quite a lot more than I'd been led to expect and it went to my head for a time. I got grand ideas about moving to the shires, where they take their hunting seriously, and ending up as Master of the Heythrop, or some damfool nonsense. I spent a week traipsing around different places and then I decided I was better off in Sussex, where I belonged. Big fish in a small pond, in other words.'

'And Winthrop and Gayford were your agents?'

'One of them. I went to half a dozen. Combed the neighbourhood, you might say, but these people had one estate on their books which sounded promising, so I made an appointment to be shown round. I'd been expecting one of the partners to turn up, in his best bib and tucker, me being such a catch, but when I arrived there was just this girl and she explained that her boss had got bronchitis or something. I was a bit miffed, to be honest with you, and anyway the place turned out to be a dud. So that was that and I hadn't given it another thought until last night in the saloon bar, when it all came back to me.'

'But this is incredible, Anthony! We seem to have been talking of nothing but Pauline ever since we came here and do you realise you're the only person I ever met who saw and spoke to her?'

'Well, don't expect anything much from that. My recollections are distinctly hazy.'

'But you must remember something, don't you? How she looked, what her voice was like? Do try!'

'She looked all right, I think. Small, fairish hair, not bad legs. Nothing special about her voice that I recall. She was very keen on riding, I do remember that.'

'I beg your pardon, Anthony! Would you mind repeating that?'

'Not at all, often as you like. I said she was very keen on riding. I think that's why she took the initiative and came out to show me round herself, instead of leaving it to one of the gentlemen clerks. She was grabbing the opportunity to talk to someone who knew a bit about horses. In fact, once we'd seen what a wash-out the house was, that was practically all we did talk about. She said I'd better take a look at the stables, just for form's sake and so she could tell her boss she'd done a proper job. They were in better nick than the living quarters, as a matter of fact and I could tell that she was pretty well informed on the subject, so I started asking her a few questions.'

'And what did she tell you?'

'Oh, about how, when she was a very young child she'd been brought up with horses and horsey people, but then for some reason she went right off it. Came a nasty cropper and lost her nerve, I daresay. Anyway, for nearly twenty years she couldn't look at a horse without feeling sick, but then quite recently a friend of hers had told her she was a silly fool. All she had to do was grit her teeth, climb into the saddle and go cantering off. In five minutes all the hang-ups would have disappeared and she'd start getting a lot more fun out of life. So that's exactly how it turned out and her only regret was that she'd wasted all those years when she could have been enjoying herself.'

'Well, thank you, Anthony, that has been most illuminating.'

'Not at all. Always happy to be of assistance.'

'I suppose she didn't happen to tell you the name of this friend?'

'Don't think so. No reason why she should. I got the impression it was a young man, but I could be wrong.'

The minute hand on my watch stood at twenty past ten and I knew that it could not be long now before Robin arrived to claim his car keys. So I did not press the point, but said:

'Never mind, you've been a great help. So much so that I now propose to do something for you in return.'

'Thanks, old girl. What's that?'

'I intend to keep my mouth shut about the fact that you did not dine off an indifferent omelette last night, or that, if you did, it was only after traipsing around Chissingfield in search of something more exotic.'

A return of the earlier expression greeted this announcement, only now there was wariness in it too, as though the transgressing stable lad was pointing a loaded gun at him. Ignoring it, I went on:

'The reason why I intend to back you up in this small deception is solely to save you embarrassment.'

'My dear Tessa, what embarrassment?'

'Of having to face some awkward questions. It was a chance in a thousand that you should have been at the Weston Arms last night, in time to hear the reporter's story, and I think it may have shaken you up a bit.'

'No, it didn't.'

'Well, perhaps not at the time, but, thinking it over when you'd gone to bed, it may have struck you that it was rather unfortunate that you had such a shaky alibi for the time when Verity was murdered.'

'No, it didn't, what rubbish! I never set eyes on the girl.'

'Yes, so you said, but on the other hand you were one of the few non-residents of Chissingfield who did set eyes on Pauline and may have done so on subsequent occasions, for all anyone knows.'

'What absolute rot! I neither saw nor heard from her again after that half hour we spent together and, anyway, she probably knew dozens of people from outside.'

'Maybe so, but perhaps none of the others was an habitue of the Weston Arms. I am right in assuming that it was your headquarters when you were down here looking at properties, and that's why you were back this time, when you found yourself without a roof over your head?'

'Well, yes, that's true enough, but it still doesn't justify all these insinuations.'

'Please understand that I'm not making them personally, I'm only pointing out what insinuations might be thrown at you, if I were to remind Robin that you were out to dinner last night. In all the excitement the landlord forgot to tell you he'd telephoned, didn't he? Otherwise, I don't suppose you'd have been quite so forthcoming about Pauline because, you see, Anthony, the sad truth is that obviously the reason why you picked a shabby place like the Weston Arms the first time was that you'd heard about the reputation of Jake and Louisa, who were then running it. And that, I must explain, is a much stronger connection than the other one you mentioned.'

'In God's name, why?'

'Because it provides the first hint of a link between the first murder and the second.'

He did not reply to this, possibly because, like me, he had seen Robin on the staircase.

'Morning, Anthony!' he said, picking up the keys, which were lying on the table. 'Looks like you've got a good day for it!'

'Not bad. Could have done with another downpour, though.'

'You're not going yet, are you?' I asked Robin.

'Not for ten minutes, but there's something I want to fetch from the car.'

'It's not locked,' Anthony told him. 'Hardly seemed necessary, with the whole place surrounded by cops. Feel like a drink, Tessa?'

'No, thanks. In any case, the bar doesn't open till eleven.'

'No, I suppose not. How about some coffee, if I can find someone to rustle it up?'

'Yes, good idea, I'll be back in a minute,' I said, getting up and giving him the chance he was searching for to escape. 'There's something I need from the car too.'

Robin was locking the boot, which he then tested, to make sure it was secure.

'Did you find it?'

'Yes, underneath the rug and mackintosh cover. I suppose he didn't think of looking that far down.'

'So that's one worry out of the way.'

'Oh, I wasn't all that worried. I guessed it would be there.'

'Yes,' I agreed, 'so did I.'

(3)

I have a system, when it comes to backing horses, which is to put my money on anything whose name has theatrical associations. It has not made my fortune yet and has been known to land me in such uneconomic ventures as backing three horses in a field of five. I stick to it, however, in the belief that consistency must pay eventually and because it provides a personal, as well as financial, interest in the outcome. Moreover, I do not consider that I lose any more by it than those who follow tipsters, or, more risky still, are knowledgeable about form.

I had explained all this to Toby, while studying our cards before the first race in the outdoor bar of the Members' Enclosure, where we had arranged to meet Robin, and he then left me there while he went to place our bets.

Two minutes later Jock Symington detached himself from a group consisting of two red-faced, confident look-ing men and one hatchet-faced, confident looking woman, and came over to join me.

'Got a nice day for it, anyway,' he remarked, waving a rolled up copy of *Sporting Life* in the general direction of the nice day. His other hand was clutching a race card and a tumbler of whisky, so I invited him to sit down. 'Thanks, I will. Your husband not here, then?'

'Oh yes, he'll be along presently. He had to stop off in Chissingfield. Toby's here too, as you saw. He's gone to join the Tote queue.'

'Ah, too bad! I've missed the bus then.'

'You mean you had a hot tip for us?'

'No, I wouldn't rate it as high as that, but if you fancy a long shot, it might be worth a flutter.'

'One of yours?'

'No, this one is trained by an ex-jockey who used to ride for me. It's only his second season, but things are coming right for him and he could have a winner here. Give us your card and I'll mark it for you.'

When he handed it back I was disgusted to find that he had put a cross against number eleven, which was called Mr Doolittle. Mindful of Jimmie's warning, I muttered:

'I think I had better find Toby and tell him about this. If Robin comes, will you say I'll be back in five minutes?'

'No, you stay here and wait for him. I'll see to it for you. Fiver be all right?'

'Oh yes, fine, thanks awfully,' I said, thinking that to lose ten pounds on the first race would not be a propitious start and, after a moment's sombre silence, Mr Symington said:

'Bad business that, at your hotel last night. I suppose that's what's keeping your husband now?'

'No, what makes you think so?'

'Oh well, the word gets around, you know.'

'I do know, but it's the wrong word. We're just visitors, here on holiday. It was a shocking thing to happen and it would be absurd to pretend it hasn't spoilt things, but there's no more to it than that. Was it Louisa who gave you the idea that he was working on it officially?'

'Not that I recall. I did speak to her on the telephone this morning, but that was about something else.'

'Oh yes, of course,' I chipped in, seizing the chance to change the subject. 'She's riding for you this afternoon, isn't she? I must say, I do admire her.'

'Admire her?' he repeated in an abstracted voice, as though thinking of something else.

'For her courage in going through with it, in spite of everything. I know I couldn't. After all, Verity was a friend, as well an employee and it can't be much fun for them, or very good for business either, but she tells me she's determined. . . .'

I tailed off here because he had closed his eyes and was shaking his head about, as people sometimes do when they are being teased by a persistent wasp. Seeing no wasp, I asked:

'Is anything the matter?'

'What? No, not really,' he replied, opening his eyes, 'just something I remembered . . . you'll have to excuse me, I'm afraid. Got to make a telephone call.'

'What have you been saying to Jock Symington to get him so steamed up?' Robin asked. 'He bellowed at me about where to find you and then swept on like a man possessed.'

'I honestly don't know, Robin. It was most peculiar. We were chatting away and he suddenly went off his head. Never mind, whatever fit has come upon him may yet save my bacon. Tell me how you got on?'

'I will, later. We'd better move now, hadn't we, if we're not to miss the first race?'

'Oughtn't we to wait for Toby?'

'Oh, he's all right. I met him coming away from the Tote. He's gone to spread himself out over a bench for three on the grass opposite the winning post.'

'Too late now, then. What a pity!'

'What is?'

'Whichever way it goes, I shall be at least one fiver down the drain.'

Mr Doolittle won by a length, at eighteen to one.

'Come along, both of you!' I said, 'champagne all round! Do you realise that if by some miracle Mr Symington backed it each way, I shall have won over three hundred pounds?'

'It is more likely that he forgot all about it,' Toby said, 'which would serve you right for being so morbidly distrustful.'

'I am not to blame for that, it is Jimmie's fault. The second time he has given me bad advice.'

'It is your fault for listening to him, though. You ought to have realised by now that he has the mind of an adolescent and judges the world and everyone in it in those terms.'

Something in this remark caused me to lose my concentration and I dropped my race card on the grass. Straightening up again, I spoke my thoughts aloud:

'Oh yes, of course, Stephanie! How stupid of me not to have seen it before. It explains everything.'

'Not to me, I must tell you. How about you, Robin?'

'I shan't try. The excitement of winning has turned her brain.'

'Not so far as to forget that you were going to tell us what passed between you and the Superintendent this morning,' I reminded him, taking a quick look round the outdoor bar, to see if Jock Symington was among those present, which he was not. 'How did it go?'

'Most of it would bore you stiff. Just a question of plod, plod, sift, sift through the evidence so far, which, as you know, amounts to less than a row of beans. Only two new facts have come to light and they both relate to Young Mr Winthrop. It seems that at some point between trying to ring me and getting run over, he formed the intention of writing me a letter.'

'I cannot cut my way through all this jargon,' Toby complained, 'I should have thought he either wrote you a letter, or he did not?'

'It's quite simple. Before he left his house for the last time he had started a letter. It consisted of half a page of shaky handwriting and was found inside a pile of papers beside his blotter. So he may not have decided whether to complete it or not. Or perhaps he had every intention of doing so, but was interrupted. It is something no one is every likely to know. Hence the jargon. Satisfied?'

'Yes, that will do. What had he written up to that point?'

'That, having heard I was back in the neighbourhood, he had attempted to ring me up, but without success and, on reflection, had decided that what he had to say would be more appropriately contained in a letter. Full stop.'

'And that was all?'

'That was all.'

'How heartbreaking for you! One more paragraph and he might have named the murderer.'

'I doubt it. If he'd had anything as sensational as that up his sleeve, I don't think he'd have kept it there all this time. It is more likely that he would have roused himself to make the trip to London.'

'So you are not heartbroken?'

'It is disappointing, naturally, but it does at least reinforce the theory that, the accident was contrived. Unfortunately, it also widens the field there. Numerous unknown people could have been aware that he was trying to get in touch with me.'

The voice on the loudspeaker by the paddock was urging the jockeys to get mounted, please, so, recalling them to business, I said:

'That means we only have five minutes left. I can't find a single horse in this race with the right sort of name. Do you think I might forget the system for once and back one called Junior Scribe? It does sound so apt.'

'Yes, it does and I should go ahead, if I were you. This is going to be your lucky day and we must all make the most of it.'

None of us had anything to celebrate after the second race, so we stayed on our bench in the sun and I reopened the conversation where it had been left off: 'When you said he might have been interrupted, was that just a guess?'

'No, there are grounds for believing it.'

'What grounds?'

'Yesterday evening, before Verity's murder was reported and most of the available manpower switched to that, Wilkins had two men on house-to-house calls, trying to piece together how Winthrop had spent his last few hours. He lived alone and looked after himself, with just a daily help, a woman named Mrs Crawley, who came for two hours every morning. So that wasn't very fertile ground, but fortunately the old lady opposite, a Miss Smiley, whose name belies her nature, is an invalid, with nothing much to pass the time but keep her eyes skinned on the house across the road. It can't provide much excitement, because Winthrop had very few visitors and kept to a regular routine. However, yesterday afternoon there was a break in the pattern.'

'What happened then?'

'He did have visitors. They arrived at about two o'clock and Miss Smiley was of the opinion that they cannot have been expected.'

'Why was that?'

'Because after lunch on Thursday he always went to the market, to stock up with supplies for the weekend. He preferred to go in the afternoon, when it was less crowded, and also it was usually possible to pick up some bargains when the stalls were beginning to close down. However, it looks as though Miss Smiley may have been wrong because the front door was opened almost immediately and the two visitors went inside.'

'Did she recognise them?'

'No, but you and Toby will. An elderly couple, he tall and white haired and she wearing a lavender coloured dress.'

'Oh, I see! The Fellowes out on their cross country tramp! How long did they stay?'

'Miss Smiley was unable to tell us that. Her masseuse had arrived in the meantime, leaving her so tired, or so relaxed perhaps, that she fell asleep until tea time.'

'So they might all have gone to the market together? Has the Superintendent asked them about it?'

'He will have by now. He telephoned the hotel while I was there, to make an appointment. Mrs Fellowes answered the call herself, which was a coincidence, unless she's been put in charge of the switchboard this morning.'

'Oh well, I daresay Louisa has gone for a gallop, to limber up for her race. Did Mrs Fellowes sound put out?'

'Not remotely. Wilkins had the impression that she assumed his business had something to do with their stolen property. Needless to say, he did not bother to disabuse her.'

'I doubt if his duplicity will do him any good,' Toby said. 'The object, presumably, was to spring it on her, before she had time to concoct some pretty story about having gone to the wrong house by mistake, but in my opinion he would need to get up earlier in the morning to catch that one out. No doubt, she'll be bored stiff, poor lady, but not half as bored as he'll be when she's finished with him. What am I to back for you in this race, Tessa?'

'Nothing, thank you. There are only two runners and it's no use backing them both because in this situation things are always so arranged that the favourite wins by a mile.'

'So why not back the favourite?'

'Because it's called Woolamoolamoo, which signifies nothing, unless it happens to be a minor character in *Hiawatha*. Also it's trained by Jock Symington, so the system could break down this time. Now that I'm rich, I'm going to be like Mr God and only bet on certainties.'

'What about My Alys for the three-thirty?' was his next question, as we studied the card once more, Woolamoolamoo having won by a mile.

'In Wonderland? It's not spelt that way and, besides, it's not strictly a play.'

'I know that, I was thinking of the girl in *Hay Fever*.'

'There isn't a girl with a name anything like that in *Hay Fever*.'

'Please yourself, but you may live to regret it.'

'We'll see about that,' I said, getting up. 'Back in ten minutes.'

I started with a tour of the outdoor bar, in the hope of being accosted by a beaming Jock Symington, pockets bulging with my winnings, but he was not there. Mr God, who was there, in the company of one of the red-faced men from the previous cast, told me he'd shortly be seeing him in the paddock and could pass on a message.

'I just wanted to thank him for his tip.'

'Paid off, did it?'

'Handsomely.'

'Good! He'll be pleased about that, if I get a chance to tell him, but he's got a lot on his plate at present. Some business going on with the stewards.'

The next stop was the Ladies' Cloakroom, which landed me in another waste of precious time. Race courses being the last stronghold of male chauvinism, no facilities are provided for the women jockeys and half the public washrooms had been partitioned off for them to change in. As a result, it was eighteen minutes past three when I came out, but there was a telephone kiosk beside the entrance, so I leapt inside and dialled a number which I had noted down in my diary a few days earlier.

Roberta answered and, realising from the signals and clanking of coins that I was in a public call box, invited me to hang up, so that Jimmie could ring me back and we could conduct the conversation with less turmoil. He did so within half a minute and I said:

'Is there a character in *Hay Fever* called A-L-Y-S?'

'No, I don't think so. No, there isn't.'

'That's all right, then.'

'Why do you want to know? Have you got a bet on it?'

'No, other way round. You're sure, are you?'

'I ought to be. I played in the damn thing eight perform-
ances a week for ten weeks.'

'Yes, so you did. Which reminds me: was it during that
tour that you met Verity? Jimmie! Are you still there,
Jimmie?'

'I don't know. I think I may have fainted. Did she tell
you . . . ? Oh, hell! Listen, Tessa, what do you think you're
doing? Trying to trap me, or something?'

'No, what I'm trying to do is profit by your father's advice.
It's the only thing I got from him, so I may as well make
the most of it.'

'What's he been telling you?'

'That the ingredients of success are ninety percent information and ten percent luck. At the moment I'm working
on the ninety, so goodbye and thanks for your help.'

'Who won?' I asked the solitary figure on the bench.

'My Alys streaked past the post three lengths ahead of
her nearest rival.'

'Oh dear, so you were right!'

'In a sense, but it will not do me any good. The horse did
very well, hardly out of breath, but the rider fell off at the
first fence and completed the journey on foot.'

'That's good! My ten percent is still keeping its head
above water. Where's Robin?'

'He said he was getting bored and would go home. To
his spiritual home, I suspect.'

'To catch up with the latest from Superintendent Wilkins?'

'Quite so. I am about ready for a sight of home myself,
my temporal one, I mean. How would you feel about leaving tomorrow?'

'I doubt if I'll be able to drag Robin away. Now that he's
getting wound up again, he's really enjoying the holiday.

He won't have much time for me, though, so I may decide to go to Roakes with you. I'll let you know this evening.'

The die was cast before that, however, because only a few minutes later the voice on the tannoy announced that the non-runner in the fifth race was number fourteen. There was no need to check it on the race card, for I had been watching the riders' names going up on the board beside the finishing post and I already knew which one was missing.

'Come on!' I said. 'And let's just hope you can remember where you left your car and we shan't find that some fool of a driver has wedged you in. There's been too much time wasted already and we haven't a minute to lose.'

By the time we found it we could hear the distant cheers and groans from the crowd we had fought our way through to get there, signifying that it was now past four o'clock.

'Do we know where we're going?' he asked, backing out on to the grass.

'Not the faintest idea, but when in doubt ask a policeman. There'll be one on point duty when we come out and he's bound to know. You can drop me off there, if you like, and go ahead to start packing.'

(4)

Half an hour later, in an office in Robin's spiritual home, I was saying: 'What a fool I was not to have foreseen it! No wonder Jock Symington behaved as though one of us had gone mad. And when you told us, Robin, that Mrs Fellowes had answered the telephone herself, that really should have clinched it.'

'And what was the significance of that?' the Superintendent enquired.

'Well, she is not one to exert herself unnecessarily and it can't then have been later than midday, nearly four hours before Louisa was due to appear in the paddock. She had told us earlier that she had nothing much to do this morning, since all the hotel guests were out for lunch and it was closed to non-residents. So the fact that she wasn't near the switchboard should have been a warning. Presumably, people would still be ringing up for advance reservations and they'd be needed more than ever now, if the hotel wasn't to go out of business.'

'One might have assumed, as Mrs Fellowes did, that she had already left for the race course.'

'Leaving no one at all in charge? She's not unprofessional in that way, only in taking on too many jobs and not having time to do more than half of them properly. Besides, until half past three, at the earliest, there would have been nothing whatever for her to do when she got there. Nowhere to sit around and gossip with the other jockeys, for instance. All the women riders were herded into a space about half the size of this room. You couldn't imagine them spending more time there than it took to change into their silks.'

'If you turn out to be right,' Robin said, 'one thing I find inexplicable is that she told Symington in advance that she would not be riding his mount. I take it that's how you account for his reaction when you told him that she would be?'

'Yes, and it would also account for Mr God telling me later that there'd been some bother with the stewards. Obviously, after I spoke to him, he'd tried to get in touch with Louisa, to warn her that the horse had been scratched and, having failed, was in terror that she would turn up, all smiles, to receive his final instructions. However, I don't find it inexplicable and I don't put it down to sportsmanship either. It's more likely that she realised that letting him know in good time would create far less sensation than just not turning up when the time came. Neither he nor anyone else had seriously expected her to ride today, so there'd have been no surprise or comment, if she hadn't. With any luck, it could have been as late as seven o'clock before anyone realised she had gone, giving her a start, I must point out, of something like eight hours.'

After a glance at the telephone by his hand, the Superintendent said:

'Well, you seem very confident about this, Mrs Price, and, as you know, I'm taking it seriously enough to follow it up. Two of my men are on their way there now, so we should be hearing something in a few minutes.'

'And I trust I shan't have wasted your time. I don't think so. There have been too many pointers along the way for today's misunderstanding not to have its place in the scheme. The only unknown quantity, in my opinion, is whether she was on her own, or whether . . .'

The sentence was never completed because his hand had jumped to the telephone, as it hiccoughed on the first ring.

COMING HOME

'What did the Fellowes have to say about their visit to Young Mr Winthrop yesterday afternoon?' I asked at dinner, which, considering she had only had two hours' notice, was well up to Mrs Parkes's standard.

'They denied it absolutely, or rather she did. Charles was hardly allowed a word in edgeways.'

'Did she get away with it?'

'She didn't do badly. When told that two people answering to their description had been seen by a reliable witness going into the house, she gave a merry trill of laughter and said: "Oh, you can't mean dear old Miss Smiley? Don't tell me she's still alive! She must be well over eighty and blind as a bat, poor dear! So sad really, these lonely old people, living in the past, as so many of them do.'''

'Was that an accurate description?'

'There was enough in it to serve her purpose, I daresay. The constable gave it as his opinion that there was nothing much wrong with her mind, but it has to be said that she didn't recognise the Fellowes by name, although she must have met them often enough. In any case, I doubt if Wilkins will think it worth pursuing now.'

'All the same, I bet it was them and it would be nice to know what took them there. Maybe I'll ask Avril one of these days. Like all good cruise passengers, we've promised to keep in touch and meet for lunch in London.

I shall put it to her that she and Charles were more worried than they wanted us to know about their possessions turning up intact after the house was burnt down and that the Godstow fire had given the knife another twist. Her taking it for granted when she answered the Superintendent's call that his business concerned stolen property, rather than murder, shows where her mind was concentrated. I shall also suggest that they had begun to be afraid that they were victims of a carefully planned fraud, whereby selected, temporarily unoccupied houses, known to contain works of art or other valuables, were first looted and then set on fire, thus ensuring that the rest of the contents would also be destroyed.'

'What would have been the purpose of that?' Toby asked. 'Why bother?'

'Obviously, one reason would be to delay for as long as possible the discovery that part of the contents was undamaged and in the hands of the master-minding fence. It was sheer chance, or maybe lack of discipline on the part of one of the thieves, hoping to set up a little private business for himself on the side, which revealed that the Fellowes' house had been burgled before it was burnt down. I can imagine that a secondary motive would have been to make it that much harder for the police to identify the gang. No finger prints, for a start, and I've heard that even the print of the blade that was used to force an entry can be a dead give-away. Besides, the really professional thieves concentrate on one particular category, such as jewellery or cash, leaving all the rest strictly alone. So this naturally gives them a sort of label and serves to narrow the field of likely culprits. Sending the whole lot up in flames would have wiped out that disadvantage and given them anonymity.'

'And you think that clever little Mrs Fellowes would have worked all this out for herself?'

'Yes, I do, and that as a consequence, in their own case at least, she had begun to be afraid that someone in her husband's firm, perhaps even one of their own sons, might have been involved, if not directly then as an innocent dupe. Naturally, she hesitated to confide such doubts and fears to Robin, knowing what that could lead to, so she decided to begin by having a chat with Young Mr Winthrop.'

'What would he have been able to tell her?'

'I'm not sure and perhaps she wasn't either, but we do know, for a start, that she'd remembered there'd been a similar incident a few years earlier and it may well have been in a house whose sale his firm was negotiating. I shall remind her that in those days Irene Gayford was his junior partner and that it was not long afterwards that his secretary was murdered.'

'To all of which,' Robin said, 'she will reply at great length and with the utmost candour and amiability, and at the end of it you will have learnt nothing more than you know already.'

'Yes, but it will be a pleasure to watch her skating over the surface and afterwards I shall reward her for her candour and amiability by assuring her that she and Charles were in no way responsible for Young Mr Winthrop's accident.'

'Why should she feel that they were?'

'It might have occurred to her that, had they not prevented his setting forth to the market at his usual time, he might never have found himself in the path of that lorry and would have returned home, safe and sound for tea. I shall explain that when she rang him yesterday morning to fix the appointment, the call was intercepted and that this, combined with the fact that he was known to have been trying to get in touch with Robin, had made his death inevitable.'

'I should be interested to know whether you suspected right from the start that Louisa was behind it. I shan't bother to ask, though, because I know you would say yes, in any case.'

'No, I couldn't do that, Toby, because once or twice I went badly astray. That was mainly your fault.'

'Yes, I knew it would turn out that you had nothing to blame yourself for.'

'It was when you were building up your case against Anthony. It shook me for a time and it shows how difficult it must be for juries to reach the right verdict. But then, when I had my talk to him this morning and he kept putting his great foot in it, I realised he was incapable of all those underhand tricks you had accused him of. Jimmie was a much worse problem.'

'Why Jimmie?'

'Because he's so much more wayward and imaginative and, allowing for that extraordinary tale about breaking into his father's house being true, it would have been in character to have tacked on the extra bit about the bloodstained shirt, in order to provide himself with an alibi for Verity's murder. At least, that's how I was afraid the Superintendent would see it; just a wild story to account for the missing half hour, and why I kept quiet about it. Things would have got completely out of hand if it had then come out that he had a motive.'

'I simply don't understand what you're talking about. How could it have come out that he had a motive for murdering someone he hadn't set eyes on until three days ago?'

'That's what we were meant to think, but it wasn't true. It was stupid of me not to have seen it the first time he walked into the hotel. I've got used to susceptible females goggling at him, but Verity's reaction was really over the top. It wasn't until I remembered that Bobbie was the other person to have uttered that doom laden phrase "two or three years ago" that anything clicked.'

'Why, what happened to her two or three years ago?'

'She almost lost the light of her life. She told me that Jimmie had fallen heavily for a girl he'd met in Bath, which is where Verity used to stay with her grandmother. She became pregnant, though, or said she had, and had expectations of marriage, which he had no intention of fulfilling. He dropped her and scurried home to mother. Irresponsible, you may say, and you'd be right, but at least Verity had plenty of money and was old enough to know her way around.'

'But I still don't understand what made you so sure that she was the girl.'

'Well, for one thing, it explained his equivocal behaviour to Stephanie. He obviously didn't care a farthing for her, but he put on a tremendous act whenever they were together in public. One theory was that it was done to ingratiate himself with his father, but, once I got the hang of it, I realised that it was much more likely to have been for Verity's benefit. His way of signalling that his affections were engaged elsewhere and it was no use her trying to re-kindle old fires. Once I'd got that sorted out, I was able to cross him off my list.'

'I would have expected it to move him to the top of your list. Supposing Verity had refused to be fobbed off so easily and was blackmailing him by threatening to tell his father that she was the mother of the Godstow grandson? That really would have been a motive.'

'No, it wouldn't. He didn't give a damn what his father thought of him. Besides, it wasn't Verity's murder that bothered me, only the fear of his getting involved in a lot of interrogation and suspicion and all the repercussions that would have brought crashing down on Bobbie. After all, it was his idea, not mine, to go into the summer house, which would have been a fatuous thing to do if he'd known she was lying dead inside it. My real fear was that he might have had some hand in the conspiracy that Pauline had got caught up in and that it was he, and not Anthony, who was parading a false excuse to keep an eye on what Robin was up to. When I saw that it was just a warning to Verity not to waste her time hanging around the stage door on her afternoon off, everything fell into place, which was a big relief. It would be hateful to think that anyone who loved cricket could be mixed up in crime.'

'So, apart from those two minor aberrations, you never put a foot wrong?'

'Oh yes, my worst failure was with Jake. If only I'd paid closer attention to what he told me on that first afternoon, when he was patching up the summer house, it would have saved endless wasted time later on. Unfortunately, I was so intent on finding ways to alleviate the tedium of the country-side that I seized on the first whiff of intrigue that was wafted my way and magnified it into a completely false situation.'

'Yes,' Robin said, 'I do remember thinking at the time that the explanation you had hit on was unworthy of you. What was it really all about, do you suppose?'

'I think Jake and Verity must have met there secretly to concoct ways and means to get rid of you and me, without actually damaging the hotel's reputation. It was soon afterwards that we had the first of that long series of minor mishaps, which I now regard as having been designed to make our lives uncomfortable.'

'I realised from the moment Jake recognised me in the dining room that I had ceased to be a favoured guest, but could he seriously have imagined that, having come here to re-open enquiries into Pauline's murder, I could be induced to drop the idea because of a radio left on all night, a dearth of coat hangers, or a faulty stove?'

'No, of course not, but I think he could have borne it better if you'd been staying somewhere else and not on his own premises. Your presence made him uneasy because he was terrified of Louisa committing some indiscretion.'

'You mean he suspected all along that she'd killed Pauline?'

'No, I doubt that. I do think he had begun to be afraid that she was mixed up in it in some way, but perhaps nothing more definite than that. Otherwise, he would never have then proceeded to hand me her motive on a plate. He could not have relied on my being so dim as not to recognise it for what it was, unless he'd failed to recognise it himself.'

'And what was it?' Toby asked.

'Oh, that she'd always had dreams of being the chatelaine of some vast country house, with her own horses in her own stables. Jake said they'd achieved it by a combination of hard work on his part and business acumen on hers, but I ask you! There they were, running a tiny pub in a seedy part of Chissingfield and serving lunch and dinner in a dining room probably no larger than this one. It would have taken them years and centuries to earn enough capital to set themselves up in that style.'

'But Jimmie told us his father was backing them?'

'He said he thought it must be so, but he got it wrong, as usual. Everything Mr God told me on the night of his birthday party made it plain that he would never have invested money in such an enterprise. The horses alone, I might tell you, eating their heads off all through the winter, would have made it totally uneconomic and he wouldn't have touched it with a barge pole wrapped in the *Financial Times*.'

'So it is your guess that she set to and raised the money in some other way? Presumably, by acting as informant to one of the more raffish customers of the Weston Arms during one of his spells out of prison?'

'Yes, and the first move was to befriend Pauline, who had access to all the right sort of knowledge. She hit on a rather brilliant way of doing it too. It would have started, I expect, when she put her name down on Winthrop and Gayford's books, as a prospective buyer. Then she got to hear about Pauline's history and it was she who talked her into laying all the ghosts by taking up riding. Anthony had the impression that it was a young man who'd done that, but I expect Pauline referred to someone called Lou, which he took to be a shortened form of Lewis. Anyway, for a time the scheme worked splendidly, Louisa getting the information she needed and passing it on to her customer and Pauline cantering over the heath for all she was worth. But then . . .'

'You must bear with me,' Toby said, 'if the tribulations of the past few days have brought me to premature senility, but what sort of information are we talking about?'

'The inside kind. Naturally, everyone for miles around knew when some grand expensive house came on the market, either for sale or rent, but in one or two cases Pauline's knowledge was far more detailed and extensive than the general one, which was quite enough for Louisa's purpose. She wasn't out for huge sums of money, just a thousand or two every now and then, to keep her solvent, when circumstances provided the right opportunity. And that was where Pauline was so useful. Every detail of position and surroundings was recorded in her office files and she knew as much about the lay-out of the rooms and what they contained as if she had walked over every inch of them herself. Indeed, as we know from Anthony's experience, she doubtless had walked over every inch of some of them, more than once. She was equally well informed about such extras as the whereabouts and movements of the owners, who had charge of the keys at any given time and how diligent such guardians were likely to be, as well as the workings of the burglar alarm system. It was a complete dossier, containing everything the successful burglar needed to know and eventually, as I was about to say, Pauline must have grasped the connection and begun to realise that there might be something fishy about this friendly interest Louisa took in all the minutest details of her job. It began to worry her and she finally found the courage to speak out. There may even have been hints that she intended to pass on the news to her employer. Anyway, she said enough to convince Louisa that she would never be safe so long as Pauline was alive.'

'But how was it done? How did she persuade Pauline to cancel the visit to her aunt and where did she go instead?'

'Oh, I think I've worked that out. By this time, you see, the money had started to roll in and she'd raised enough to get her hands on Mattingly Grange. There was still a lot more needed for conversion and so on, but in the meantime she and Jake were doing what they could by way of decorating and putting the garden in order, in their spare time. Obviously, their headquarters during this period would have been the flat over the stables, but owing to the demands of their calling they could never both be there at the same time for more than a few hours. So the day came when she told Jake she intended to take a couple of days off and get stuck into some big job, but would be back on Friday, in plenty of time for the race meeting rush. All this, I must remind you, was ten days before Pauline's murder was discovered.'

'And what would she have told Pauline?'

'Suggested that she should spend part of her holiday at the flat and, in return for a little home decorating, which we know to have been one of her accomplishments, Louisa would lay on an intensive course of riding and jumping. She would hire a couple of hacks and they would set off at dawn, when no one was about to catch them at it. It had to be kept a secret, you see, because Pauline hadn't told any of her other friends about this new craze of hers. She was still afraid of breaking down and losing her nerve, which would have left her feeling more humiliated than ever. What, of course, happened is that Louisa picked her up on her way to the station, as arranged, took her to the flat, finished her off and during the night heaved her into the Land Rover and deposited her on the heath, covered by a sheet of tarpaulin. The next morning she turned up, bright and smiling, to resume her duties at the Weston Arms. What do you think of that?'

'Not bad!' Robin admitted. 'It would fit with most of the known facts, but I regret to say that you have left one gaping hole in it. It does nothing to explain why Verity was murdered.'

'Oh well, of course,' I said, aware that this part of my reconstruction still required a little polishing, 'I should have thought that was self-evident. Obviously, the money was running out and Louisa had reverted to old habits and contacted former friends. Hence the fire at Heavenly

Towers. Somehow Verity got wind of what lay behind that and was threatening to make a nuisance of herself. Something like that, anyway. That curious remark Louisa made this morning, when she brought our breakfast trolley up, finally convinced me. She said something about the murderer returning to the scene to look for his hat and gloves, almost as though she were picturing it in her mind, although, as far as I know, we're the only three people, apart from the police, who know about the gloves.'

Neither of them looked over-impressed by this explanation, but luckily I was saved by the bell. The telephone rang and Toby, who would be happier if it had never been invented, requested me to go to the hall and answer it.

'I'll go,' Robin said, 'I'm expecting a call.'

He was out for nearly ten minutes and when he returned he said:

'They've found Louisa. She hadn't got very far.'

'Where?'

'About three miles away. Hanging from a branch in the woods. They think she must have stood up on the saddle to reach it. The horse was unharmed. It had started to come home on its own, but someone managed to catch it before it strayed on to the road.'

'So I was right?'

'It would appear so. For what it's worth, Jake swears that he knew nothing about it, until a few days ago, when the Godstow fire set him thinking. In Wilkins's opinion, he was finding it all too easy by then to believe the worst of her because the marriage was cracking up, anyway.'

'Oh, why was that?'

'Because she was becoming increasingly obsessed, to the exclusion of everything else, by her *folies de grandeur*. She would have sacrificed everything and worked them both into the ground rather than give up Mattingly Grange, and he was sick to death of it. He'd been much happier with his saloon bar and bijou restaurant at the Weston Arms. Furthermore, a new element had entered his life and that's where you made your glaring mistake. It ought to teach you never to look for a complicated solution, in preference to the obvious one.'

'What ought to teach me?'

'You were right the first time. He had fallen in love with Verity. How far she reciprocated these feelings is not known, perhaps not quite so fervently once she had seen Jimmie again, but Jake had already told Louisa that he was leaving her and wanted a divorce. That did it, of course. She'd have known that she hadn't a hope of keeping the place going without him and all her life's dream would have turned to ashes.'

'So Verity had condemned herself to death, just like Pauline?'

'It could never be proven, I daresay, but that's what Jake believes and he maintains that he'd made it clear to Louisa last night that he had no intention of standing by her. She could have six clear hours to get away and then he would go to the police. So there it is and only the last big question remains.'

'Which one is that?' Toby asked.

'After we've collected our belongings from Numbers Two and Three tomorrow morning, where shall we spend the rest of our holiday?'

'And with an extra three hundred pounds to squander!' I reminded him, 'Mr Symington having turned out to be a goodie, after all. It is going to need some thought.'

'Although, if you were to take my advice, which you all too rarely do, you would stay at home and spend your money on some new curtains or improving books. Wouldn't you imagine, Robin, that even Tessa has had enough turmoil and tragedy to keep her going for a week or two?'

'You shouldn't bank on it and I certainly shan't. I'm another who means to take a leaf from Mr God's bible and in future I shall only bet on certainties.'

THE END

FELICITY SHAW

THE detective novels of Anne Morice seem rather to reflect the actual life and background of the author, whose full married name was Felicity Anne Morice Worthington Shaw. Felicity was born in the county of Kent on February 18, 1916, one of four daughters of Harry Edward Worthington, a well-loved village doctor, and his pretty young wife, Muriel Rose Morice. Seemingly this is an unexceptional provenance for an English mystery writer—yet in fact Felicity's compli-cated ancestry was like something out of a classic English mystery, with several cases of children born on the wrong side of the blanket to prominent sires and their humbly born paramours. Her mother Muriel Rose was the natural daugh-ter of dressmaker Rebecca Garnett Gould and Charles John Morice, a Harrow graduate and footballer who played in the 1872 England/Scotland match. Doffing his football kit after this triumph, Charles became a stockbroker like his father, his brothers and his nephew Percy John de Para-vicini, son of Baron James Prior de Paravicini and Charles' only surviving sister, Valentina Antoinette Sampayo Morice. (Of Scottish mercantile origin, the Morices had extensive Portuguese business connections.) Charles also found time, when not playing the fields of sport or commerce, to father a pair of out-of-wedlock children with a coachman's daughter, Clementina Frances Turvey, whom he would later marry.

Her mother having passed away when she was only four years old, Muriel Rose was raised by her half-sister Kitty, who had wed a commercial traveler, at the village of Birchington-on-Sea, Kent, near the city of Margate. There she met kindly local doctor Harry Worthington when he treated her during a local measles outbreak. The case of measles led to marriage between the physician and his patient, with the couple wedding in 1904, when Harry was thirty-six and Muriel Rose but twenty-two. Together Harry and Muriel Rose had a daughter, Elizabeth, in 1906. However Muriel Rose's three later daughters—Angela, Felicity and Yvonne—were fathered by another man, London playwright Frederick Leonard Lonsdale, the author of such popular stage works (many of them adapted as films) as *On Approval* and *The Last of Mrs. Cheyney* as well as being the most steady of Muriel Rose's many lovers.

Unfortunately for Muriel Rose, Lonsdale's interest in her evaporated as his stage success mounted. The playwright proposed pensioning off his discarded mistress with an annual stipend of one hundred pounds apiece for each of his natural daughters, provided that he and Muriel Rose never met again. The offer was accepted, although Muriel Rose, a woman of golden flights and fancies who romantically went by the name Lucy Glitters (she told her daughters that her father had christened her with this appellation on account of his having won a bet on a horse by that name on the day she was born), never got over the rejection. Meanwhile, "poor Dr. Worthington" as he was now known, had come down with Parkinson's Disease and he was packed off with a nurse to a cottage while "Lucy Glitters," now in straitened financial circumstances by her standards, moved with her daughters to a maisonette above a cake shop in Belgravia, London, in a bid to get the girls established. Felicity's older sister Angela went into acting for a profession, and her mother's theatrical ambition for her daughter is said to have been the inspiration for Noel Coward's amusingly imploring 1935 hit song "Don't Put Your Daughter on the Stage, Mrs. Worthington." Angela's greatest contribution to the cause of thespianism by far came when she married actor and theatrical agent Robin Fox, with whom she produced England's Fox acting dynasty, including her sons Edward and James and grandchildren Laurence, Jack, Emilia and Freddie.

Felicity meanwhile went to work in the office of the GPO Film Unit, a subdivision of the United Kingdom's General Post Office established in 1933 to produce documentary films. Her daughter Mary Premila Boseman has written that it was at the GPO Film Unit that the "pretty and fashionably slim" Felicity met documentarian Alexander Shaw—"good looking, strong featured, dark haired and with strange brown eyes between yellow and green"—and told herself "that's the man I'm going to marry," which she did. During the Thirties and Forties Alex produced and/or directed over a score of prestige documentaries, including *Tank Patrol*, *Our Country* (introduced by actor Burgess Meredith) and *Penicillin*. After World War Two Alex worked with the United Nations agencies UNESCO and UNRWA and he and Felicity and their three children resided in developing nations all around the world. Felicity's daughter Mary recalls that Felicity "set up house in most of these places adapting to each circumstance. Furniture and curtains and so on were made of local materials. . . . The only possession that followed us everywhere from England was the box of Christmas decorations, practically heirlooms, fragile and attractive and unbroken throughout. In Wad Medani in the Sudan they hung on a thorn bush and looked charming."

It was during these years that Felicity began writing fiction, eventually publishing two fine mainstream novels, *The Happy Exiles* (1956) and *Sun-Trap* (1958). The former novel, a lightly satirical comedy of manners about British and American expatriates in an unnamed British colony during the dying days of the Empire, received particularly good reviews and was published in both the United Kingdom and the United States, but after a nasty bout with malaria and the death, back in England, of her mother Lucy Glitters, Felicity put writing aside for more than a decade, until under her pseudonym Anne Morice, drawn from her two middle names, she successfully launched her Tessa Crichton mystery series in 1970. "From the royalties of these books," notes Mary Premila Boseman, "she was able to buy a house in Hambleden, near Henley-on-Thames; this was the first of our houses that wasn't rented." Felicity spent a great deal more time in the home country during the last two decades of her life, gardening and cooking for friends (though she herself when alone subsisted on a diet of black coffee and watercress) and industriously spinning her tales of genteel English murder in locales much like that in which she now resided. Sometimes she joined Alex in his overseas travels to different places, including Washington, D.C., which she wrote about with characteristic wryness in her 1977 detective novel *Murder with Mimicry* ("a nice lively book saturated with show business," pronounced the *New York Times Book Review*). Felicity Shaw lived a full life of richly varied experiences, which are rewardingly reflected in her books, the last of which was published posthumously in 1990, a year after her death at the age of seventy-three on May 18th, 1989.

Curtis Evans

CPSIA information can be obtained
at www.ICGtesting.com
Printed in the USA
LVHW030904250621
691134LV00002B/176

9 781914 150272